KRISTEN PARKER

When Shadows Breathe Beneath the Moon

This book was professionally typeset on Reedsy.
Find out more at reedsy.com

Contents

One

The Moonlit Meeting

The moon was full, a silver lantern casting its glow over the vast expanse of the world. The shadows that clung to the trees in the distance seemed to stretch and pulse, as if they were alive, swaying under the weight of the night. In the village of Althra, nestled at the edge of the Darkwood Forest, the night air felt heavier than usual. An inexplicable tension gripped the land, like the moment before a storm breaks—silent, anticipatory, and fraught with danger.

Mirella stood at the edge of the village square, the hem of her cloak swishing softly against the cobblestone streets. Her dark eyes scanned the horizon, her pulse quickening as the wind stirred the air. There was something in the wind tonight. Something... *wrong.* She had felt it for days, a whisper of shadow creeping into her dreams, a presence that seemed to follow her wherever she went. It had started as fleeting glimpses, distorted shapes in the corners of her vision, but now, it was growing stronger—louder. It was as if the shadows themselves were beckoning her, calling her to them.

"Too many nights like this," she murmured under her breath, her fingers tightening around the pendant she wore around her neck, an heirloom from her mother—a relic she had never fully understood.

Her dreams had been more vivid lately—strange, cryptic visions of monstrous creatures, darkness swallowing the light, and a chilling, unrecognizable voice. The fear in those dreams was real, an oppressive weight that clung to her even after she woke. And tonight, beneath the light of the full moon, that fear was creeping into the waking world.

The quiet village of Althra was a peaceful place, where the worst trouble usually came from a wayward storm or the occasional disagreement between neighbors. But tonight, there was a stillness in the air that made her skin crawl. It was as though the earth itself was holding its breath.

Mirella turned her gaze toward the forest, her heart skipping a beat as she noticed something in the distance—movement. A silhouette, darker than the night itself, slinking between the trees at the edge of the village. A figure, tall and silent, but something about it felt wrong. She had been walking these paths for years, and she knew the forest well, yet tonight, something lurked there that shouldn't be.

Was it the shadows?

Her thoughts spiraled, but before she could move, the village was engulfed by an unnatural stillness. The air grew thick, oppressive. A ripple of cold swept through her, a chill that made her bones ache. The wind had ceased, and in that eerie silence, the distant sound of footsteps crunching the underbrush reached her ears.

Mirella's breath caught. She wasn't alone.

Her instincts screamed at her to run, but her feet remained planted, unwilling to tear her gaze from the edge of the forest. The figure from the trees stepped forward, its form taking shape in the moonlight. It wasn't human—at least, not entirely. Its features were sharp, angular, its skin the color of midnight shadows, but its eyes—those eyes—glowed a feral, blood-red hue.

A cold dread settled in the pit of her stomach. *What are you?* Her hand unconsciously clutched the pendant tighter, as if its presence could shield her from the encroaching dark.

But before she could take another breath, the creature surged forward, a low, guttural growl emanating from its throat. Mirella's heart skipped in panic, her body frozen in place as the creature drew closer.

And then, a flash of movement—too fast to fully register.

A figure appeared at her side, seemingly out of nowhere, dressed in dark, weathered armor. A warrior, tall and lean, his face hidden beneath the hood of a cloak. Without a word, the stranger stepped forward, drawing a long, curved blade from his side with the practiced ease of one who had spent years in battle. His presence was commanding, like a force of nature. He stood between her and the creature, his body tense, waiting for the next move.

"You're in the wrong place," the man's voice rang out, low and steady, with an accent she couldn't place.

The creature paused, eyes narrowing, before it let out a chilling hiss. With a speed that defied reason, it lunged. The man reacted instantly, his sword slicing through the air in a deadly arc. The clash of steel rang out through the silence, a spark of light flashing in the darkness. The creature recoiled, but it was not finished. It snarled and circled, its glowing eyes never leaving the stranger.

Mirella stood frozen, her heart pounding in her chest. *Who is this man?* She could feel the pull of his presence, strong and steady, like the earth beneath her feet, grounding her amidst the chaos. But she didn't know him, had never seen him before. He was an enigma, a shadow amongst shadows.

The creature launched another attack, and the man met it with skill and precision, his movements fluid and purposeful. The clang of their battle echoed in the still night. Mirella's hand found its way to her waist, where a dagger she'd inherited from her mother hung, but her mind raced—there was nothing she could do. She was a healer, not a fighter.

Then, the man shifted, his movements a blur, and in one swift motion, he thrust his blade into the creature's chest. It screeched in agony, thrashing wildly as it tried to free itself, but it was already too late. With one final shudder, the creature collapsed to the ground, motionless.

For a long moment, the only sound was the heavy breathing of the man, his sword still raised. Mirella's eyes widened as he turned toward her, the hood falling back, revealing his sharp features and the strange intensity in his eyes. There was something unmistakable about him, something that stirred a memory deep within her, but she couldn't place it.

He studied her for a moment, his gaze intense but unreadable. There was a flicker of recognition there—just a fleeting moment, but it sent a shiver down her spine.

"Are you alright?" His voice was a low, gravelly whisper, but his words carried with them an undeniable force.

Mirella nodded, her mouth dry. "I... I think so. Who... are you?" The words tumbled out, her voice shaky as the adrenaline wore off, leaving her weak in the knees.

The man's lips twitched slightly, though it wasn't quite a smile. "Riven," he said simply, his gaze never leaving hers. "I've been looking for you."

Mirella felt a strange tug at her chest. "Looking for me?" She repeated, the tension in her chest growing. "Why?"

Riven's expression hardened, as if considering whether to speak further, but after a long silence, he finally spoke, his voice quieter now, almost reluctant. "Because it's not just the creatures you need to fear. There's something much worse coming. And your blood is the key to stopping it."

Mirella's heart skipped a beat, her breath catching in her throat. She had known for years that something darker was coming, but this? This was something far worse than she had ever imagined. The shadowy creatures were only the beginning.

And the stranger—Riven—was the only one who seemed to know what was happening. But why did it feel as if their paths were already written, that they were somehow connected by something beyond their control?

He stepped closer, lowering his sword, his dark eyes never leaving hers. "It's not safe here," he said, the urgency clear in his tone. "Come with me. There's much you don't understand yet. And I don't think we have much time."

Without waiting for her response, Riven turned, already moving toward the dark woods. Mirella hesitated, her gaze shifting between him and the dark creature still crumpled on the ground. The night had been altered. Her world had changed in the span of a few heartbeats.

As if driven by some unseen force, she followed.

The shadows had already begun to stretch longer, and

though the silver moon still bathed the earth in its light, there was a chill that lingered—one that could not be chased away.

Riven's steps echoed through the silence, each one carrying him deeper into the unknown. And with each step, Mirella felt the pull between them grow stronger.

In the distance, the trees seemed to whisper their secrets, and for the first time, she realized that the future she had been running from was now unfolding before her. And in the heart of it all stood the man she barely knew, yet somehow, deeply trusted.

Riven was the key to unraveling the mystery that haunted her, but the questions were only beginning. Would she be ready for what was to come?

The answers, it seemed, were waiting under the watch of the moon.

Riven's steps led them deeper into the heart of the forest. The path was narrow, barely visible under the thick canopy of trees, and the air grew heavier with each step they took. The silver moonlight barely pierced the dense branches overhead, casting long shadows that seemed to whisper in the wind, their voices unintelligible yet unnerving. The forest was alive, not just with the rustling of leaves but with something older, something darker, and Mirella felt it in her bones.

She hurried to keep up, her feet stumbling over the uneven ground. The air was thick with the scent of damp earth and decaying leaves. Despite the coolness of the night, her skin prickled with warmth, and she couldn't shake the feeling that eyes were watching her from the shadows. The village had always been safe, peaceful, but now, nothing felt certain.

Riven didn't speak, but she could feel the tension radiating off him. His movements were purposeful, as though every step was calculated. His cloak rustled with his swift pace, and the silver light reflected off the hilt of his sword, gleaming like an ominous promise. The fight earlier had been swift, efficient— almost too much so. Mirella couldn't help but wonder just how much he knew about these creatures, and how much he was keeping from her.

Finally, after what felt like an eternity, they reached a small clearing. The moonlight bathed the space in a pale, ethereal glow, and for a moment, it was the only sound—the soft whisper of the wind, the rustle of distant trees. Riven stopped and turned to face her.

Mirella caught her breath, heart pounding in her chest. The clearing felt… different. It wasn't just the shift in atmosphere, but the weight of something ancient in the air—something that tied the land and the magic of the world together. The air hummed with power, and Mirella could feel it tugging at her soul. She didn't know what it was, but it felt familiar—like a memory she hadn't fully recovered yet.

"Why did you bring me here?" Mirella asked, her voice small, barely above a whisper, but it still seemed to carry through the night. Her gaze darted from Riven to the shadows that lingered just beyond the clearing's edge.

Riven's eyes were fixed on her, intense and unreadable. "Because the answers you seek are here. And you are not the only one being hunted."

The words hit her like a cold wave, and her breath caught in her throat. Her pulse quickened, and she instinctively reached for the pendant at her neck again, the cold silver almost grounding her, but it didn't ease the panic that crept through her veins.

"I don't understand," she murmured. "You said my blood is the key to stopping this. But... why me? Why now? Why—"

Riven cut her off with a sharp look. "Because you carry more than just your mother's blood. The shadows that follow you, the creatures, the nightmares—they're not random. They're drawn to you because of what's inside you." He paused, his expression hardening. "Because you are the descendant of a powerful bloodline that was lost long ago. And the time has come for it to return."

Mirella's heart skipped. "What do you mean?"

Riven stepped closer, his gaze never leaving hers, and this time, there was a flicker of something softer in his eyes—a mixture of warning and something else she couldn't quite place. "The bloodline you carry, Mirella... it is bound to the moon. The very moonlight that calls to you, that ties your dreams to the shadows, is connected to your ancestry. You were born for this moment—whether you believe it or not. You are the key to breaking the curse that's been locked away for centuries."

She felt a cold wave of realization wash over her. Her mother's strange warnings, her dreams that never quite made sense, the way the moonlight had always felt different to her— *it was all connected.* But how? Why hadn't she known this before?

"Then... you know what the creature is, don't you?" she asked, her voice trembling, the memory of the shadow still fresh in her mind.

Riven nodded, his face shadowed with grim understanding. "Yes. That creature... it is a harbinger of the Night King. He is the one who controls the shadows. The one who has cursed your bloodline."

"The Night King?" Mirella repeated the name, her voice

distant, as if the words themselves carried a weight she wasn't sure she was ready to bear. "But… you said it was a curse. What do I have to do with it?"

Riven's lips pressed into a thin line. "The curse is tied to you because your bloodline is the only one that can either undo it—or complete it. The prophecy is not a simple story. It's a choice, a battle, and a sacrifice. You must choose: either you sever the bond that connects you to the darkness… or you embrace it and let it consume you. Either way, the balance will be tipped."

Mirella felt a sickening twist in her stomach. "You're saying that I have to *choose* whether to end everything?"

Riven's silence was all the answer she needed.

Her pulse raced, and her thoughts were a whirlwind. She was caught between the man in front of her, whose eyes held secrets and half-spoken truths, and the overwhelming power that pulled at her from within the forest—the dark pull of shadows, the weight of fate. The urge to run was overwhelming, but she knew better now. Running would only delay the inevitable. The darkness wouldn't let her escape.

"Tell me what to do," she whispered, her voice shaking with both fear and resolve. "What must I do to stop this?"

Riven's eyes softened, and for the briefest moment, she saw something raw, something human in him. Something she hadn't expected.

"First, you must face what is inside you." His voice was low, heavy with meaning. "The darkness you fear, the monsters from your dreams, they are a part of you, just as much as the light is. Only by embracing both can you break free. Only by accepting your true power can you set things right."

Mirella shook her head. "You don't understand. I can't

embrace darkness. I'm supposed to—"

"To heal," Riven finished for her, his voice taut with the weight of his own pain. "But even healers must sometimes embrace the shadow. Otherwise, you will never truly heal anyone."

The words hung in the air, and for a long moment, neither of them spoke. Then, Riven's eyes grew colder again, and the shift was palpable. Whatever warmth had been between them was gone, replaced with the grim reality of their situation.

"You have two choices," he said quietly. "The first is to stand by and allow the darkness to consume you, to allow it to take everything you love. The second is to fight. And that fight begins now. The choice is yours. But know this… I will not let you face it alone."

With that, he turned sharply, heading deeper into the clearing. Mirella felt her heart leap in her chest. She was drawn to him—compelled to follow him, even though the future was uncertain and the darkness loomed closer than ever.

Her mind screamed at her to stop, to run, but her feet moved of their own accord, carrying her into the unknown with Riven leading the way.

And so, beneath the watchful gaze of the silver moon, Mirella knew she had crossed a threshold. There was no going back.

Two

The Veil Between Worlds

The journey had taken them farther from the safety of the village than Mirella had ever ventured before. The winding path led deeper into the forest, where the trees grew thicker and their branches wove together, blocking the moonlight. The air grew heavier, thick with a strange, almost palpable energy, as though the very earth beneath their feet held its breath, waiting for something unseen to unfold.

Mirella's heart pounded as she walked beside Riven, her steps reluctant, yet drawn to him by an unspoken force. The tension between them had only grown since the night in the clearing. She hadn't asked him why he'd chosen to protect her or what his true intentions were, but the magnetic pull she felt toward him was undeniable. Each time their eyes met, a charge of energy passed between them—unnerving, electric. And yet, it was the fear of the prophecy, of the dark forces creeping closer, that kept her moving forward. She could feel it in her bones;

something was coming. And there was no turning back now.

"How much farther?" Mirella asked, her voice quiet but urgent. Her gaze flicked nervously to the path ahead, where shadows stretched unnaturally long, creeping like living things.

Riven didn't look at her as he answered, his eyes fixed on the path. "We'll be there soon."

His voice, while steady, carried an edge of tension that didn't go unnoticed by Mirella. He seemed distant, lost in his own thoughts, and yet, his every movement was purposeful. His sword was sheathed at his side, but Mirella knew he was ready for anything. His presence, once a comfort, now felt like an armor he couldn't shed. And the deeper they ventured into the forest, the more she understood that he wasn't just protecting her from the monsters of the night—he was running from something, too.

She glanced at him, studying his profile. The moonlight caught the hard angles of his jaw, the faint scars that marked his skin, and the determination in his eyes. He was a warrior, a man forged by battles and loss. But beneath it all, something inside of him—something buried deep—felt like it was unraveling.

The path narrowed as they descended into a ravine, and the forest seemed to close in on them. The trees were ancient here, twisted and gnarled, their bark dark and slick as if they had witnessed centuries of secrets. A strange quiet hung in the air, the usual sounds of the forest stilled by an unseen force. Mirella's breath quickened, and she instinctively clutched the pendant at her neck. The silver chain felt cold against her skin.

"Riven…" she whispered, her voice carrying a hint of fear. "What did the seer mean? That my bloodline is connected to this darkness…"

Riven's pace slowed, his eyes flicking to her for a brief moment. There was something in his gaze—something softer than the soldier she had come to know. But the moment passed quickly, and the hardness returned. He continued walking, his steps sure, but his jaw clenched.

"You're asking the right questions now," he said, his voice low. "But you may not like the answers."

Mirella swallowed hard, the weight of his words sinking in. Every step she took felt heavier than the last, the air around her thickening as if the world itself were pressing against her. But she didn't stop. She couldn't.

Ahead, a clearing appeared in the shadows, its edges defined by a ring of jagged stones. At the center stood an ancient stone structure—a small, weathered hut, barely visible beneath the dense canopy. From where they stood, it seemed as if the hut had been forgotten by time itself. The door was ajar, as though inviting them in.

Mirella's breath caught in her throat. The feeling of dread that had been building in her chest intensified. This was the place, she realized, the place where the answers lay buried.

"We're here," Riven said, his voice barely a whisper as he approached the door. He didn't wait for Mirella to follow, but she knew better than to hesitate. She had no choice but to step into the unknown.

She stepped through the door after him, the air inside thick with the scent of herbs and dust. The hut was dim, lit only by a single, flickering candle on a table cluttered with strange trinkets and objects Mirella didn't recognize. The walls were lined with shelves of jars, dried plants, and scrolls of ancient parchment. It was a place that felt as though it existed between worlds—a threshold between the mortal realm and something far older, far darker.

At the far side of the room, a figure stirred. An old woman, hunched and wrapped in layers of tattered cloth, her long silver hair flowing around her face like a veil. Her eyes, though clouded with age, were sharp and knowing. She smiled faintly as Riven and Mirella entered.

"Ah," the woman rasped, her voice thick with the weight of years. "The chosen ones. I've been waiting for you."

Mirella felt a chill run down her spine, the words landing with an unsettling truth. She wasn't sure what to expect from the seer, but this woman was not what she had imagined. There was something both ancient and terrifying in the way the old woman regarded them—an understanding of the world that stretched beyond time.

"You know why we're here?" Mirella asked, her voice faltering slightly. She stepped forward, her eyes never leaving the seer's.

The woman chuckled, the sound low and haunting, as though it had been caught in the webs of ages long past. "Of course. But there is no simple answer, child. Not when the world is at the cusp of unraveling."

Mirella felt her heart tighten. Riven moved to stand beside her, his presence a steadying force, but even he seemed unsure, his gaze flickering uneasily toward the seer.

"You've come because the veil between worlds is thinning," the woman continued, her gnarled hands trembling as she gestured to a stone bowl beside her. "The darkness you both fear is not just an enemy. It is an ancient force that seeks to erase everything—the light, the moon, the very fabric of what makes this world whole."

Mirella's pulse quickened. "And what does that have to do

with me?"

The old woman's eyes gleamed with something both sympathetic and grave. "It has everything to do with you, child. You are the key. Your bloodline has been cursed for generations, tied to the moon's light and the shadows that feed on it. The prophecy is clear: only the silver light of the moon can seal the darkness, but only if the chosen ones, those who are bound by fate, embrace their bond completely. You and him, Mirella." The seer's gaze shifted to Riven. "Together, you must become one with the darkness to defeat it. But only if you can accept that what lies between you is not just fate… but something far older. Something far deeper."

Mirella's heart skipped. "Our bond?"

The old woman nodded slowly. "Yes. The prophecy does not just ask you to fight the darkness—it asks you to embrace it, to merge the light within you with the shadows you both fear. You are the moon's chosen, and he"—she gestured to Riven—"is tied to the shadows that threaten to consume it."

Mirella turned to Riven, searching his face for any sign of recognition, any hint that he understood what the seer was saying. But his expression was unreadable, distant.

"Why is it always us?" Mirella whispered, almost to herself. "Why are we the ones who must carry this burden?"

The seer smiled again, though it was more sorrowful this time. "Because you, child, have the strength to choose. The choice will not be easy. And it will cost you both more than you can imagine."

Riven finally spoke, his voice low and intense. "What is it we have to do?"

The seer's eyes gleamed, as though she had been waiting for that question. "You must step beyond the veil. There is a place where the worlds meet—the edge of the known and the unknown. It is there that the true battle will take place. But to get there, you must first unlock the power within yourselves. The bond that ties you two together is not a mere connection of hearts. It is a binding of light and shadow, a force older than time itself. Only when you accept that truth will you be able to stop the darkness."

Mirella's chest tightened as the weight of the words settled over her. *Light and shadow.* She glanced at Riven again. Could she truly accept the darkness within her? Was the bond between them strong enough to withstand what was coming?

The seer's voice cut through her thoughts. "The barrier between worlds is thinning, child. And when it breaks, the darkness will flood this world. You must make your choice—now."

Mirella's heart raced. The air around her hummed with tension, the weight of the prophecy pressing down on her like a physical force. She turned to Riven, her eyes searching his. What did he feel? Did he understand this as she did, or was he also trapped in the uncertainty of their fates?

Riven's eyes locked with hers, and for the briefest moment, all the chaos of the world seemed to fade away. There was something in his gaze—something raw, something vulnerable—that made her heart race with the weight of what was at stake. He was as much a part of this darkness as she was, yet somehow, his presence grounded her.

"Together," he whispered, almost as if he were reassuring himself as much as her. "We face this… together."

The seer nodded. "You have made the first step. The veil is about to tear open. Prepare yourselves."

And with those final words, the air grew cold, and the room

seemed to shift. The boundaries between the world they knew and the unknown beyond seemed to blur, and Mirella could feel the ground tremble beneath her feet.

The darkness was coming. And the veil between worlds was about to break.

And it was only a matter of time before they would have to make their choice.

The air in the hut seemed to thicken as the seer's words hung in the heavy silence. Mirella felt a shiver crawl up her spine, the room itself seeming to bend with the weight of prophecy. Her pulse thudded in her ears as the world outside faded into a blur, swallowed by the intensity of the moment. Riven's hand brushed against hers, a fleeting connection that sent a ripple of warmth through her. The quiet reassurance in his touch didn't quell the storm brewing inside her—it only intensified it.

The seer's ancient eyes gleamed, and Mirella felt an unsettling shift in the energy around them. The walls, the shelves of jars and scrolls, the flickering candlelight—all of it seemed to pulse with a rhythm she couldn't quite place. It wasn't just magic; it was something deeper, something darker, something that gnawed at the edges of her mind.

"The darkness is near," the seer said softly, as though merely stating the inevitable. "You must act quickly. It will come for you both. Not just as creatures of shadow, but as the very fabric of the curse itself. The prophecy will not wait."

The seer's voice, while soft, had a biting edge to it, and Mirella felt as if each word was a weight pressing down on her chest. The urgency in the air was suffocating. She turned toward Riven, her heart catching in her throat. His expression was grim, his brows furrowed as if he were weighing something deep in his mind. Mirella knew that he understood the gravity of the situation—perhaps more than she did.

But the bond between them was still an enigma. She didn't know how to fully grasp it, how to wield the power she could barely comprehend. What did the seer mean by embracing the darkness? Was that even possible without losing herself?

Riven's hand was on his sword now, his fingers curled around the hilt with a familiarity that made Mirella's chest tighten. The sword wasn't just a weapon; it was an extension of him—his heritage, his burden. Her heart clenched as she realized that Riven wasn't just trying to protect her; he was also fighting against something far darker, something that had followed him for his entire life.

"How do we stop it?" Mirella found her voice, her words sharp and desperate.

The seer's gaze flickered briefly to Riven before returning to Mirella. "You must go to the Rift. The place where the worlds bleed together. It is where the barrier thins and where the shadows are strongest. The moon's silver light may be your only weapon, but it is useless if you do not understand what you must do with it. The two of you must embrace the balance between light and shadow."

Mirella felt her breath catch, and for a moment, she could not speak. "Embrace the balance?" she repeated, her voice shaking. "What does that even mean?"

The seer's lips curled into a knowing smile, but it wasn't comforting. "It means you must accept both the light and the shadow within you. The moon's light flows through your bloodline, but it is not a gift—at least, not the way you think. And Riven's darkness is not a curse, but a part of him, just as you are a part of the prophecy."

Mirella's eyes flicked to Riven, but he stood motionless, his gaze unwavering. She couldn't read him in that moment—he was a stranger, a warrior caught in the snare of his own past, yet also her only ally in the battle ahead.

"I don't understand," she whispered.

"You will," the seer replied, her voice dipping into something ancient. "But not until you stand at the Rift. Until you face what lies between these worlds. Only then will you know the truth of your bond. Only then will you be able to stop the darkness from consuming everything."

The ground beneath them suddenly trembled, and the candlelight flickered erratically. Mirella's breath quickened, and she took a step back, her heart racing. The air felt different now—charged, as though the seer's words had opened a door to something much larger than they could have anticipated.

Riven's hand shot out to steady her, his grip firm around her arm. "We have to move," he said urgently. His voice was low, strained with the pressure of what was to come. "Now."

Mirella nodded, swallowing her fear, though the weight of the prophecy pressed heavy against her chest. She wanted to run—wanted to find some corner of the world where she didn't have to face the inevitable. But she couldn't. Not anymore.

The seer's voice was soft but insistent, her words trailing them as they made for the door. "Beware, Mirella. Beware the shadows that seek to deceive. The Rift will test your very soul."

Riven didn't wait for more; his steps were quick, his eyes already scanning the darkened path ahead. Mirella followed him out into the cold night air, the full moon above casting an eerie, silvery glow across the forest floor. The clearing behind them seemed to breathe, the shadows warping as if alive, stretching toward them.

Mirella glanced behind her, half-expecting the darkness to chase them, but it didn't. For now, the shadows were silent, still—but she knew that was only temporary. They were running out of time.

The path ahead was shrouded in mist, a thin veil of fog that seemed to swirl around them as if trying to pull them deeper into the woods. The deeper they went, the more the forest seemed to close in on them. The trees whispered in voices too low to understand, and the wind howled as if warning them of the danger ahead. There was no comfort here, only the chilling certainty that the barrier between worlds was thinning.

Riven moved faster now, his steps sure and quick, as though he knew exactly where they were headed. Mirella struggled to keep up, her heart pounding with fear and anticipation, the weight of the prophecy heavy on her shoulders. The air was thick with magic, with something old and potent that seemed to vibrate in her very bones. Her mother's pendant grew cold against her chest, and she reached for it instinctively, hoping it would offer her some form of protection. But it was as if the world itself was rejecting her attempts to grasp control.

They reached the edge of the forest, and the trees parted to reveal a vast chasm—its edges bathed in the faint, eerie glow of the moon. The Rift.

Mirella's breath caught as she gazed into the abyss. The ground seemed to ripple, the air thick with dark energy. At the very edge, the fabric of the world seemed to twist and stretch, a tear between realms that pulsed with an otherworldly glow.

Riven stepped forward, his body tense, his eyes fixed on the Rift. He didn't look back at her, but Mirella knew—this was it. The final choice.

Without warning, the air around them trembled, a low hum vibrating through the earth beneath their feet. The shadows along the edge of the Rift began to stir, crawling toward them like hungry tendrils, coiling and twisting in the moonlight.

"It's happening," Riven muttered, his voice tight with fear and determination. "The barrier is breaking."

Mirella's chest tightened as the Rift pulsed once more, sending a wave of power through the air. She could feel it in her bones, the way the world was shifting, changing. Time itself seemed to bend, and for a moment, she lost herself in the sensation. The air grew thick, as though they were standing on the precipice of reality itself.

Then, the shadows surged forward. The dark shapes twisted and roared, their forms indistinct but terrifying. They were no longer creatures of flesh and blood, but embodiments of the very darkness that had been creeping toward them for so long. And now, it was here.

Riven raised his sword, his grip steady, as he stepped in front of Mirella. His posture was rigid, his stance protective, but even he seemed unsure of what was coming.

"Stay close," he ordered, his voice sharp.

Mirella nodded, her heart racing as she took a step closer to him. The darkness was closing in, but they were here, together, at the center of it all. And in that moment, the bond between them was undeniable.

As the shadows closed in, Mirella braced herself, the realization settling in: this was their fight now. The future, the prophecy, the world—they were all entwined with her and Riven. She had no choice but to face it.

The moonlight pulsed with an ancient power, the last light between them and the void.

And then, as the shadows lunged, everything went black.

Three

The Shadow's Kiss

The moon hung high in the sky, casting its silver glow across the forest floor, where the trees seemed to sway as if whispering to one another. The night was unusually still, the kind of stillness that pressed in on you, making each breath feel heavy, as though the earth itself was holding its breath, waiting for something to unfold.

Mirella stood at the edge of a clearing, her heart beating faster than it had any right to. The air was thick with magic, the kind that curled and twisted in her chest like an ache she couldn't escape. Beside her, Riven moved with silent grace, his figure shrouded by the shadows of the trees, his every step purposeful and deliberate. It was as if the very ground beneath him yielded to his presence, as if the forest recognized him as part of its darker, hidden fabric.

They had been traveling for hours, journeying deeper into the wilderness, away from the village and its familiar warmth.

With every step they took, the night seemed to close in around them, its silence more pronounced, more oppressive. Mirella's mind buzzed with questions—about the prophecy, about her bloodline, and about the bond that had already begun to take root between her and Riven. But there was one question that refused to leave her: **Why did she feel so drawn to him?**

She turned to him now, her eyes tracing the sharp outline of his profile, the faint outline of his jaw, the curve of his lips, set in determination. There was something primal in the way he moved, something untamed, as though he were part of the darkness that surrounded them. And yet, there was an undeniable pull between them—a connection that couldn't be explained by mere fate.

It was more than fate.

"Where are we going?" Mirella's voice broke through the heavy silence, shaky but steady. Her fingers gripped the pendant around her neck, the silver cold against her skin.

Riven didn't immediately respond, his eyes locked on something beyond her, somewhere far into the distance. He seemed lost in thought, his face a mask of uncertainty. When he finally spoke, his voice was low, thick with meaning. "To the edge of the world."

The words hung between them like a promise. Mirella didn't know what it meant, but she felt it deep in her bones. It was as though she had always known this path would lead them here, but she could never have predicted the depth of the pull between them.

"How much longer?" she asked, her heart a strange mixture of excitement and dread.

"Not far now," Riven answered, his voice soft but firm.

The quiet was broken only by the rustling of leaves in the

wind, the distant chirp of nocturnal creatures. Mirella could feel the weight of the world pressing down on them, the heavy cloak of magic that hung over them like a storm cloud. The moment felt suspended in time, as though everything was holding its breath, waiting for the inevitable.

Riven turned toward her, his gaze piercing, as if searching for something in her eyes. The tension between them was thick, a subtle, invisible thread that pulled tighter with each passing moment. His lips parted as though to speak, but the words seemed caught in his throat. Instead, he stepped closer to her, closing the distance between them, his presence overpowering.

Mirella's breath hitched, her body reacting before her mind could catch up. She wanted to pull away, wanted to keep some semblance of control, but there was something in his eyes that made it impossible to resist. His hand reached for her, his fingers brushing against her cheek, a simple touch that sent a jolt through her body.

"Riven…" Her voice cracked, barely a whisper against the growing intensity in the air.

"Trust me," he murmured, his voice raw and low, a command wrapped in vulnerability. His eyes darkened as he leaned in closer, his breath hot against her skin.

Mirella's heart pounded, her pulse racing as their faces hovered inches apart. She could feel the magnetic pull, the overwhelming desire to close the distance, to give in to the connection that had been building between them. She closed her eyes, her breath shaky, her lips parted as she waited for him to bridge the gap between them. And when he did—when their lips finally met—it was like a storm breaking free.

The kiss was fierce, consuming. His lips were urgent against hers, as if the entire weight of the world had fallen onto this single, fleeting moment. The shadows around them seemed to pulse, as though the very night itself responded to their kiss. Her hands moved on their own accord, reaching for him, pulling him closer, as if her body knew what her mind hadn't yet fully realized—that this was the moment, the point of no return.

And in that moment, the world around them shimmered.

A sudden flash of silver light danced across the clearing, too bright to be the moonlight alone. The very air seemed to crackle, charged with an unseen force that made the hairs on the back of her neck stand on end. The kiss, which had felt so right, was interrupted by a searing sensation that ripped through her—pain, sharp and sudden, cutting through the moment like a blade.

Mirella gasped, pulling away, her hand flying to her chest as the burn spread across her skin. It wasn't just the kiss—it was *something else*, something that marked her, a sigil that had appeared without warning. Her fingers brushed against the skin at the base of her neck, and the heat intensified, the sigil glowing faintly beneath her fingertips.

"What's happening?" she whispered, her voice trembling, her body shaking from the force of the strange magic coursing through her.

Riven stepped back, his face twisted in pain. His breath was shallow, his chest rising and falling in quick bursts as he stared at the mark on her skin, the sigil glowing faintly in the moonlight. His jaw tightened, and for a moment, his eyes flickered with something darker, something she couldn't quite place.

"It's the mark," he said, his voice rough with something close to regret. "The bond... it's not just between us. It's tied to the curse that's been haunting your bloodline. The kiss—" He stopped himself, the words heavy in his mouth. "I should have known better."

Before Mirella could ask what he meant, the air shifted. The once-still forest erupted in an unnatural noise—a screeching, guttural sound that seemed to come from every corner of the clearing at once. The shadows around them thickened, twisting, and forming into something more solid, more dangerous. The sigil on Mirella's skin burned even hotter, as if responding to the force that was coming for them.

"Riven," Mirella gasped, her voice rising in panic as the shadows took shape. A creature emerged from the darkness— its form a mass of writhing tendrils and glowing eyes. It was monstrous, a creature from her nightmares, its very presence suffocating. The same shadowy creature that had attacked her village.

Riven's hand shot out, grabbing her wrist, his grip tight as he pulled her toward him. His sword was in his hand in a blur of motion, the silver blade catching the light of the moon as he stood before her, a protector, a warrior. "Stay behind me," he ordered, his voice hard, but there was a flicker of fear in his eyes. Fear that spoke of a past he hadn't shared with her.

The creature lunged, its gaping mouth full of sharp, jagged teeth. It moved with terrifying speed, its eyes locked on Mirella, its movements almost too fast to follow. Riven's blade met it with a clash, the force of the strike sending a shockwave through the air. The creature reeled back, its shrill scream reverberating through the forest, but it didn't retreat. It was relentless, fueled by the darkness that had spawned it.

Riven swung his sword again, but the creature slithered away, its form shifting, melting into the shadows as though it were one with the night. Mirella's heart raced as the creature circled them, its eyes gleaming with hunger.

"Riven," she whispered, panic rising in her chest. "What is this thing? How do we stop it?"

Riven's jaw clenched. "It's drawn to you, Mirella. The sigil—" He glanced at her neck, where the mark was now glowing fiercely in the moonlight. "It's more than just a bond. It's a sign that the darkness knows you. And it's coming for you."

The creature lunged again, but this time, Riven was ready. With a powerful swing, he severed the creature's tendril, sending it howling into the darkness. But it wasn't enough. The shadows were thickening again, and Riven's sword was no longer enough to keep them at bay.

"Stay close," Riven barked, his voice taut with urgency. "I won't let them take you."

But the creature was only the beginning. Mirella felt it now—the weight of the curse, the bloodline that tied her to the darkness, the mark on her skin that would not fade. And as Riven turned toward her, his face filled with resolve, she knew this was only the start of something far worse.

A shadow stretched across them both, the mark on her skin burning brighter in response.

And together, they faced the darkness, not knowing if they would survive the night—or if the shadow that had claimed her bloodline would finally claim them both.

The night seemed to close in around them, suffocating, as the air pulsed with the sound of distant whispers—dark, swirling voices that seemed to come from the very trees, the very earth beneath their feet. The creature's growls echoed in the distance, its presence still looming despite the temporary reprieve. Riven's sword gleamed in the moonlight, but even its bright edge seemed dimmed by the growing shadows.

Mirella's pulse raced, her breath coming in sharp, shallow bursts as the sigil on her skin burned hot, a steady, pulsating heat that was impossible to ignore. It spread through her, deep into her veins, as though it were tying her to something far greater than she could comprehend. Her fingers traced the mark absentmindedly, feeling its sharp edges beneath her skin as though it were alive. But that was not the only thing she felt. No, the mark wasn't just some emblem of fate—it was a *part* of her now. It thrummed with an eerie power, one that was not entirely hers, but one that was pulling at her in ways she couldn't control.

The shadows on the edges of the clearing shifted again, swirling like liquid darkness. They weren't just creatures— they were manifestations of the curse that had haunted her bloodline for generations, twisting and writhing with the intent to devour. And they were coming for her.

"Riven," she whispered, her voice barely audible over the rising wind, "what does this mean? The sigil... the shadows... they're *after* me. I—"

Riven's gaze hardened, and his grip on his sword tightened. "You're not just marked by fate, Mirella. The sigil—the bond between us—it's been sealed by the curse itself. And I... I'm tied to it, too." He turned his head slightly, his eyes flickering with something like regret, but it was gone as quickly as it had appeared. "I knew it wouldn't be easy to protect you, but now it's more than that. We are connected, entwined, through this magic. Through this curse. And it's pulling us toward a choice we don't understand yet."

Mirella shook her head, trying to grasp his words through

the fog of fear clouding her thoughts. "A choice? What choice?"

Before Riven could answer, the creature surged from the shadows with a roar that made the ground tremble. Mirella barely had time to react before Riven moved, his sword slicing through the air in a swift, practiced arc. The creature recoiled, its spindly limbs twitching as it hissed, an unnerving sound that seemed to crawl into her bones.

It was smaller now, but its eyes—those glowing, blood-red eyes—burned with hunger, and the sight of them made her heart lurch with a strange mixture of dread and inevitability. The darkness wasn't just coming for her. It was coming for both of them, and no matter how much Riven fought, no matter how hard he tried to protect her, it was clear that this battle was one neither of them could win with mere weapons.

"Get back," Riven growled through clenched teeth, position-ing himself between her and the creature. His body was tense, his movements sharp as he slashed again, narrowly missing the creature's writhing form.

The shadowy creature was faster than any creature of flesh and bone, its limbs twisting and reforming as it darted in and out of the patches of darkness. The moonlight flickered, as though the very light around them was dimming in response to the shadow's power.

Mirella's heart raced in her chest as she watched, helpless, the curse that bound her to this nightmare playing out in real time. The sigil burned hotter, as if urging her to act, to do something—*anything*—to stop the creature.

Before she could fully process what was happening, a thought seized her mind with a terrifying clarity. The bond. The power that thrummed through her veins—it was hers to command. But how?

"Riven!" she shouted, her voice raw with desperation. "We need to work together. I—I can feel it, the magic inside me. It's tied to the darkness, isn't it? We need to use it, to turn it against the shadows!"

Riven glanced over his shoulder, his gaze sharp. For a moment, doubt flickered in his eyes, but it was replaced by a grim determination. "No. This magic is not something you can control. Not yet."

"You don't get it!" she cried out. "It's *inside* me. I can feel it. I have to try."

Without waiting for a response, Mirella stepped forward, her hands outstretched, palms open to the cold night air. The sigil burned hot beneath her skin as she focused on the power she now knew she carried within her—the same dark magic that tied her bloodline to the shadows.

The air around her began to shimmer, the wind picking up with unnatural force, as if the very elements recognized the power she was awakening. The ground beneath her feet trembled, and the creature hissed in fury, its eyes narrowing as it saw the change in her.

Riven stepped back, his sword still raised, but his eyes locked onto her with a mixture of awe and terror. "Mirella, stop! You don't know what you're—"

But it was too late. The shadows around her grew thicker, as if the very night were responding to her. The sigil on her skin flared to life, the glow turning a fierce, almost blinding silver. It was as though the moon itself had poured into her veins, wrapping her in its radiant light, yet it was still tainted with the darkness that she had come to understand was a part of her.

Mirella's voice broke the silence. "I'm not afraid of you."

With a final breath, she drew the power deep within her, pulling it from the darkness itself, and the world seemed to bend. The air pulsed with the force of her power as the sigil on her skin glowed bright enough to light the entire forest.

In an instant, the darkness recoiled. The creature screeched, its twisted body writhing as the moonlight intensified around Mirella, forming a barrier of light and shadow. She could feel the energy coursing through her, the power rising inside of her. It was overwhelming, and yet it felt *right*.

The creature lunged again, but this time, the shadows twisted around it, pulling it backward, restraining it in the thickening night. The creature fought against the force, its eyes filled with pure rage. But it was trapped, bound by the very darkness it had sought to consume.

Riven watched, his breath held, his sword lowered. His expression was a mixture of disbelief and wonder. "Mirella…"

The creature let out a final, horrific screech as the shadows suffocated it, pulling it into the earth like an unwilling sacrifice. And then, silence. The air cleared. The oppressive weight that had settled over the forest lifted, leaving behind a strange stillness.

Mirella collapsed to her knees, her hands trembling as the energy drained from her. The sigil faded, but the mark on her skin remained, burned into her flesh as a reminder of what had just happened. Her body ached from the exertion, but there was something else, too—a deep, unsettling sense that the battle was far from over.

"Did I… did I do it?" she whispered, looking up at Riven, her voice weak.

Riven approached her, his expression unreadable, but there was something softer in his gaze. He knelt beside her, his hand resting gently on her shoulder, his touch grounding her in the aftermath of the magic. "You did. But this… this is only the beginning. The darkness is still out there, and it knows you're capable of more than just holding it back."

Mirella swallowed hard, her chest tight. "I don't want to be part of this. This isn't me."

Riven's eyes softened, though a shadow still clung to his face. "It's part of who you are, Mirella. Whether you accept it or not. We're tied to it now—the moon, the shadows. We can't outrun it."

Her heart hammered in her chest, the realization of their fate settling on her like a heavy cloak. The bond between them was more than just shared power—it was a thread woven through the very fabric of the curse. And the shadow creatures? They were only the beginning.

Riven stood, offering her his hand. She took it without thinking, her fingers curling around his. And for a moment, she felt something shift—a deeper connection between them, something that went beyond magic. It was as if their souls were intertwined in ways she couldn't explain.

"We'll face this together," Riven said, his voice steady. "No matter what."

Mirella nodded, her body still trembling with the aftershock of the magic. But she knew one thing now—there was no turning back. The shadows were part of her, part of them, and whatever lay ahead, they would face it side by side.

As they stood together, the moonlight above seemed to shimmer once again, its pale light casting long shadows across the forest. The path before them was uncertain, but there was no denying that the darkness was not finished with them yet.

And neither was their journey.

Four

Into the Darkwoods

The moonlight was growing thinner, as if the earth itself was holding its breath. The night air pressed in with an eerie stillness, the forest around them seemingly holding the weight of an ancient secret, its dense shadows thickening as they ventured deeper into the unknown.

Mirella's steps felt heavy on the forest floor, her boots sinking slightly into the damp earth with each movement. Every crack of a twig, every rustle of leaves, seemed to vibrate with an unnatural energy. The further they traveled into the Darkwoods, the more the trees began to change. The trunks grew wider, the bark twisted in strange, spiraling patterns, and the leaves above them fluttered in ways that seemed deliberate—intelligent, even.

She could feel it now—the pulse of the forest. An ancient heartbeat. A force older than time itself, wrapping itself around her, pulling at her mind like an invisible tether. The magic here was thick and primal, woven into the very air they breathed. It was beautiful, and it was dangerous.

Riven walked ahead of her, his dark figure framed by the pale moonlight that still fought to break through the dense canopy. He was quiet, his movements fluid, the tension in his shoulders evident even from this distance. Mirella had known something was off since they had left the clearing where the creature had attacked, but it was here, in the heart of the Darkwoods, that she felt it most acutely. The fear, the urgency, the sense that something more malevolent was waiting for them.

She had thought that what happened in the clearing, the sigil on her skin, the dark power that pulsed inside her, had been the worst of it. But the forest was pulling at her, digging deep into her soul, reminding her that the true danger had only just begun.

"Riven," she called, her voice cutting through the silence.

He didn't turn around, but his pace slowed, as if he had heard the quiet tremor in her voice. "We're almost there," he said, his voice low, filled with a calm that seemed out of place against the growing tension. "Just stay close."

She couldn't help it—her gaze shifted to the shadows surrounding them. The woods felt alive with an ancient presence, the air thick with magic, like the land itself was feeding off their presence. The sense of being watched was overwhelming.

"Why here?" Mirella asked, her voice barely above a whisper. "Why bring me to the Darkwoods? What are we looking for?"

Riven stopped for a moment, his back still to her, his hand gripping the hilt of his sword. He was silent for a moment too long, and Mirella could sense his inner conflict, though it was impossible to tell if he was hiding something or simply lost in his own thoughts. When he finally spoke, his words were weighed down with more than just the gravity of their situation.

"There are answers here," he said, turning slightly to meet her gaze over his shoulder. "The Night King's power grows with every passing day. This is where it began—where it all started."

A chill crept up her spine, and her breath caught in her throat. The name sent ripples of fear through her. "The Night King…"

"Yes," Riven's voice was clipped, as if saying the name aloud made it more real, more dangerous. "He's not just a monster of legend, Mirella. He's real. And he's been waiting."

"Waiting for what?"

Riven didn't answer immediately, his gaze shifting into the distance, past the twisted trees, as though searching for something just beyond the horizon. Finally, he spoke again, his words like a cold wind.

"Waiting for you. For us."

Mirella's stomach tightened. She wasn't sure if she could trust Riven's words completely—not yet—but there was a truth in his eyes, something raw and unspoken. It was then that she realized the weight of their bond wasn't just tied to the shadows, to the magic that had marked her—it was tied to Riven's past as well. Something in his bloodline, something dark and powerful, was awakening. And she was bound to it.

Before she could speak again, a faint rustle sounded from deeper within the forest. Mirella's heart skipped a beat. Riven's hand immediately moved to his sword, his body tensing as he scanned the trees. His eyes narrowed, and she could see the muscles in his jaw flex.

"There's something here," he muttered under his breath, though his voice was barely above a whisper.

Mirella swallowed, the hair on the back of her neck standing on end. Her eyes darted to the darkened forest around them, the shadows creeping closer with each passing second.

Another rustle. This time, louder.

Riven moved first, drawing his sword with a swift, practiced motion. He didn't look back at her but gestured for her to stay behind him. Mirella's heart thudded painfully in her chest as she instinctively took a step closer to him.

"Stay sharp," he warned, his voice low, almost a growl.

Suddenly, a figure stepped into the clearing ahead of them, a silhouette barely visible in the dim light. Mirella froze, her breath catching in her throat. The figure was tall, cloaked in dark robes that seemed to ripple in the shadows themselves. Its face was obscured by a hood, but the air around it shimmered with an unnatural, cold energy.

Riven stiffened. His grip on the sword tightened, his muscles coiling in readiness. Mirella could sense his unease, the way the air around him seemed to hum with a dark, unsettling force.

"Mirella," Riven murmured, his eyes not leaving the figure. "Do not speak. Do not move."

The figure stepped forward, its face still hidden. But as it did, the shadows seemed to move with it, parting around its form like a living thing. It was as if the forest itself had bent to the figure's will.

"Mirella… and Riven." The voice that emerged from beneath the hood was low, gravelly, but with a strange clarity. "The time has come. The prophecy is unfolding."

Mirella felt a chill run through her veins. Her instincts screamed at her to run, but she remained rooted to the spot, unable to tear her eyes away from the figure that was both terrifying and familiar.

Riven stepped forward, his sword raised in a defensive stance, his eyes narrowing. "Who are you?"

The figure's hood shifted slightly, revealing a faint glimmer of something beneath it—pale skin, sharp features, and eyes that gleamed with an unsettling golden light.

"I am a messenger," the figure replied, its voice soft yet commanding. "Sent to deliver a warning."

"Warning?" Riven's voice was sharp, disbelief coloring his words. "From whom?"

The figure's lips curled into a small smile, though there was no warmth in it. "From your bloodline, Riven. From the Night King."

Mirella's pulse quickened. The words hit her like a punch. The Night King was real, and this figure—this *messenger*—was tied to him. The air between them thickened with tension, the magic crackling like an electrical storm.

"The curse is not just an ancient tale," the figure continued, its gaze flicking toward Mirella. "It is alive. It is growing. The darkness… it seeks you both. And soon, you will be forced to make a choice."

"What choice?" Riven demanded, his voice hard with a mixture of anger and confusion.

The figure remained silent for a moment, its head tilting as if considering the question. "The choice of power," it finally said. "The choice of fate. To claim what is yours—what has always been yours—or to allow the world to fall into the hands of the Night King."

Mirella's chest tightened, the weight of its words settling in like a dark cloud. Her eyes darted to Riven, but he was as unreadable as ever. The bond between them—the dark magic, the shadows—wasn't just about her bloodline. It was about *him*, too. Riven's past, his lineage, his destiny—they were all tangled up in this, tied to her in ways she couldn't yet understand.

The figure stepped closer, its presence now oppressive, the shadows swirling around it like a living cloak. "The prophecy speaks of two hearts. But those hearts must decide: will you embrace the darkness and wield it? Or will you sever the bond and doom yourselves to a life of isolation?"

Riven's grip on his sword tightened, his jaw clenched. "You speak in riddles. What do you want from us?"

The figure reached up, slowly pulling back its hood, revealing a face that was pale and strikingly beautiful. But it was not a human face. It was almost ethereal, its features sharp and unnatural. Its eyes glowed with that same unsettling gold, and its lips barely moved as it spoke again.

"I want nothing from you. But the world does. The Night King is coming, Riven. And this time, he will not be stopped."

With a sudden motion, the figure turned and began to fade into the shadows, its form dissolving as if it had never been there at all.

Riven stood frozen for a moment, his breath ragged as he sheathed his sword, the weight of the encounter pressing heavily on his shoulders. Mirella could see the tension in his body, the way his muscles were locked in place, his gaze distant.

"What was that?" she asked, her voice trembling.

Riven didn't answer immediately. He stared into the darkness where the figure had been, his eyes clouded with thoughts he wouldn't share. Finally, he turned toward her, his expression unreadable, but something in his eyes softened—just for a moment.

"The Night King's power is growing, Mirella," he said quietly. "And the choices we make—together—will determine whether we survive what's coming."

She nodded slowly, the weight of the words settling in her chest. They were bound to the prophecy, to the darkness, and the shadows that had once been distant nightmares were now closing in on them. And no matter how much she wanted to escape it, she knew deep down that there was no running from their fate.

The forest around them seemed to hold its breath, the air thick with anticipation. The Night King was not just a myth. He was real. And Mirella and Riven were the key to everything.

The journey into the Darkwoods had only just begun. And with each step they took, they were drawing closer to something far more dangerous than either of them had ever imagined.

The forest around them had fallen eerily quiet after the figure disappeared, leaving only the sound of their breathing to break the stillness. Mirella stood in the same spot, her heart pounding as her thoughts raced. The message the figure had delivered lingered in her mind, its weight sinking deeper with every passing second.

Riven was already several paces ahead of her, his hand gripping the hilt of his sword as though it were the only thing keeping him grounded. Mirella hesitated before following, the words echoing in her head like an ominous refrain: "The Night King is coming… The choice of power."

She had never asked for any of this. The magic that swirled within her, the sigil on her skin, the darkness creeping into her life—none of it had been her choice. But now, standing in the heart of the Darkwoods, the weight of her bloodline pressed down on her. And with it, the bond between her and Riven, a bond that had only deepened since their encounter with the shadows. The prophecy spoke of two hearts, two souls connected, and somehow, she knew that their fates were as intertwined as the ancient roots of the forest around them.

The trees ahead seemed to loom larger, their gnarled branches twisting like hands reaching toward the heavens. The deeper they ventured, the more oppressive the atmosphere became. The shadows felt alive here, each step forward drawing them closer to a power older and darker than anything she could comprehend.

Riven stopped abruptly, his eyes scanning the path ahead. Mirella took a cautious step forward, her gaze flicking to him. His jaw was set, his lips pressed in a tight line, but there was something in his eyes—a flicker of unease that he hadn't shown before.

"We're getting closer," Riven muttered, his voice low. "This is where it started. The magic… it's thicker here."

Mirella felt the subtle shift in the air, the crackling energy that buzzed through her skin. The shadows, too, seemed to respond to Riven's words. The leaves beneath their feet whispered and crunched, not from the wind, but from the weight of something unseen moving just beyond their reach.

"What started here?" she asked, taking a cautious step closer to him. "Riven… What's really going on? What is it about your bloodline?"

He stiffened at her words, his gaze flickering toward her for just a moment before he turned his eyes back to the path ahead. "I didn't want you to get caught up in this," he said, his voice almost a whisper. "I wanted to protect you. From the truth."

Mirella's heart sank. "The truth about what?"

Riven's shoulders tensed, and he let out a long, slow breath. When he finally spoke, his words were heavy, laden with something she couldn't name. "The Night King isn't just a creature of darkness. He's a manifestation of the curse that haunts my bloodline. My ancestors made a bargain with him long ago. They were promised power—immortality in exchange for their souls, and the souls of those who would come after. That's how I was born, Mirella. The magic that runs through me is tied to him. And every generation of my family is marked by it."

Mirella's breath caught in her throat, her mind struggling to make sense of the revelation. The curse that had been the root of so many nightmares, the darkness that had twisted her own bloodline, had also claimed his. She reached out instinctively, her fingers brushing against his arm in a gesture she hoped conveyed more than just her sympathy.

"You... you're tied to him?" she whispered, her voice trembling. "To the Night King?"

Riven's jaw clenched, and he nodded, his gaze fixed ahead, as if he couldn't bear to meet her eyes. "Yes. And this bond isn't something I can escape. It's why I've fought so hard to protect you—to keep you away from it. Because if the Night King fully awakens, if the curse consumes both of us..." His voice faltered for a moment, and for the first time, Mirella saw the vulnerability in his eyes. "I'll lose you. We'll both lose everything."

A chill crawled down Mirella's spine. The weight of Riven's words pressed down on her like a suffocating fog. They were bound to the curse, to the darkness. There was no escaping it. But she couldn't turn away now—not after everything that had already happened. She couldn't leave him.

Riven's eyes flicked to her briefly, catching the silent determination in her gaze. "You don't know what you're asking for," he said quietly. "You don't know the consequences of what we might have to do. We'll have to face the Night King head-on. And it's not just a battle for survival—it's a battle for our souls."

Mirella's heart ached at the thought of losing Riven, of losing everything. But the pull between them—the connection, the bond—was undeniable. It wasn't just about the prophecy, or the curse, or the shadows; it was about them, together. Whatever happened, they would face it side by side.

"I'm not afraid," she said firmly, her voice steady despite the storm swirling inside her. "I've already seen too much. Felt too much. You're not facing this alone. We're in this together, Riven."

He looked at her then, his eyes softening, the briefest flicker of gratitude crossing his features. But it was gone as quickly as it came, replaced by the cold resolve that had defined him since they'd first met. The forest, the magic, and the curse were closing in on them. And now, more than ever, they had to face the darkness—together.

Without another word, Riven began moving again, his steps purposeful. Mirella followed closely, her thoughts still swirling, but her resolve hardening. The air around them thickened, the shadows crawling up the trees, reaching toward them like dark fingers. She could feel the magic twisting around them now, tugging at her, making her skin tingle with an energy she could neither control nor fully understand.

As they moved deeper into the Darkwoods, the trees became even more twisted and gnarled, the branches snarled like clawing hands. The ground beneath them was uneven, the underbrush thick and tangled. The moonlight grew dimmer with every step they took, and the oppressive darkness closed in around them. Mirella could feel the shadows shifting in the corners of her vision, moving with a life of their own.

Then, it came.

The first vision.

A sudden, flickering image burst into Mirella's mind—vivid and strange. She saw a figure, a tall, shadowy shape with glowing eyes, standing in a place that seemed to shift with the flickering of the shadows. It was a man, or something like a man, but his face was obscured by a dark hood, and the air around him shimmered with a sickly aura of blackness. She could hear whispers—low, unintelligible words that echoed in her head, but there was something familiar about the image. A sense of recognition. And then, the shadowed figure reached out toward her, its hand elongated, fingers twisting like dark tendrils, and the ground beneath it cracked, sending waves of darkness toward her.

Mirella gasped, staggering backward, her hand flying to her forehead. She blinked, and the vision vanished, leaving only the cold chill of dread lingering on her skin.

Riven stopped abruptly in front of her, his eyes flashing with concern. "What's wrong?"

"I—I saw something," she breathed, her voice trembling. "A shadow… a figure. The Night King."

Riven's face hardened, his eyes narrowing with a mix of fear and determination. He reached for her, his hand gripping her shoulder. "Mirella, listen to me. This place—it's playing tricks on your mind. The Darkwoods are full of illusions, of things that aren't real. The Night King's power is ancient, and the deeper we go, the stronger the magic becomes."

But Mirella's heart was still pounding in her chest, the vision haunting her like a nightmare. "No, Riven, this felt real. It *was* real." Her voice shook as she said it, the echo of the vision still reverberating in her mind. "He's coming. He's *close*."

Riven's grip on her shoulder tightened, his gaze flicking to the dark, twisting trees around them. "I know. But we have to keep moving. We can't stop now."

She nodded, though the fear gnawing at her insides was almost unbearable. The shadows were closing in, and it felt as though time itself was unraveling with each step they took. They were moving toward something—something they couldn't escape.

And there was no turning back now.

They had entered the heart of the Darkwoods, where the veil between worlds was thinnest, and the Night King's influence was strongest. Mirella could feel it now, the weight of their connection to the curse, to the magic of the forest, pressing down on them.

With every step, the forest seemed to grow darker, more suffocating. But despite the fear clawing at her throat, Mirella found herself unwilling to turn away. She was bound to this fate, to Riven, and to the shadows that had already begun to shape her destiny.

Ahead of them, the trees parted, and in the distance, the faintest light gleamed through the darkness. But it wasn't the moon. It was something else—something ancient, something powerful, waiting for them.

And they were getting closer.

The Night King was waiting.

Five

Beneath the Silver Tree

The deeper they ventured into the Darkwoods, the more the forest seemed to swallow them whole. The trees towered above, their twisted limbs reaching out like jagged claws, blocking out the remnants of the moonlight. The ground beneath their feet was uneven, the soil thick with roots that seemed to shift and curl as if they had a life of their own. The air, too, was dense, suffused with the faint scent of damp earth and the overpowering stench of decay, as though the very woods were rotting from the inside out.

Mirella could feel the magic surrounding them now, thicker than it had ever been before. It hummed in the air, electric and ancient, prickling against her skin with every breath. The sigil on her chest, the mark left by the kiss that had bound her to Riven, burned faintly beneath her clothes. The intensity of it had only grown since they entered the heart of the Darkwoods, and with each step, her connection to Riven seemed to pull tighter, drawing them closer to something neither of them fully understood.

But what was waiting for them? The forest was silent, too silent, as though it was waiting for something to unfold. Every shadow, every movement, seemed to pulse with anticipation, as if the trees themselves were alive—watching, waiting.

"Mirella," Riven said quietly, his voice cutting through the tension that had settled between them. His steps were sure, but his gaze flickered to her, his expression unreadable. "We're close."

She nodded, though her heart beat faster at his words. She had no idea what to expect, but she could feel the weight of the moment. The deeper they went into the forest, the more the air seemed to shift around them. The silence was now almost suffocating, and the weight of something ancient and powerful pressed down on her chest, making each breath harder to take.

Riven had been distant for hours, lost in his thoughts, his face set in that familiar mask of stoic resolve. But Mirella could see it—the flicker of unease that crossed his features when he thought she wasn't looking. He wasn't just fighting the darkness that surrounded them. He was fighting something inside of himself—a battle between loyalty, duty, and the strange, undeniable connection that had been forged between them.

Then, as they rounded a bend in the path, the trees parted to reveal a clearing, and Mirella's breath caught in her throat.

At the center of the clearing stood the silver tree.

It was unlike anything Mirella had ever seen. Its bark gleamed in the dim light, silvery and smooth, as if it had been polished by the hands of time itself. Its branches twisted upward, reaching for the sky, and its leaves shimmered with an ethereal glow. The air around it was thick with an ancient energy, and the ground beneath it seemed to hum, vibrating with power.

Mirella could feel it—feel the magic emanating from the tree, calling to her. There was something about it, something deep inside her that recognized the power it held. It was as if the tree itself was a part of her, a part of something far older than she could ever understand.

"Is this it?" she whispered, her voice barely audible, as if speaking too loudly would disturb the fragile stillness of the moment.

Riven stepped forward, his eyes narrowing as he studied the tree. He didn't answer immediately, but the look in his eyes was one of recognition—a knowing that sent a shiver down Mirella's spine.

"This is the Silver Tree," Riven said at last, his voice hushed, almost reverent. "It's ancient—older than any of the other trees in the Darkwoods. It's the source of the power that binds the magic here."

Mirella took a step closer, her fingers trembling as she reached for the tree, her gaze fixed on the shimmering leaves. As her hand brushed against the bark, a sharp pulse of energy surged through her. The world around her seemed to tilt for a moment, and then everything grew still.

In that moment, the magic of the tree flooded her senses. Her heart raced, and a strange warmth spread through her chest, as if something inside her had been awakened. Visions flashed before her eyes—fragmented and fleeting, like pieces of a puzzle she couldn't yet put together. She saw herself, standing beneath the silver tree, but there was something different about her. Her eyes were glowing, and her skin was marked with the same sigil that now burned on her chest.

Then, there was Riven. His face was twisted in pain, his eyes filled with desperation as he reached for her. But there was something else—something dark—lurking behind his gaze. She saw a shadow, thick and malevolent, creeping from the ground beneath his feet. And then, the vision shifted, and she saw a figure—tall, cloaked in darkness, with eyes that glowed a burning red.

It was the Night King.

The vision shattered, and Mirella stumbled back, gasping for air as the images left her head spinning. She could feel the weight of them—the darkness, the power that had surged through her—clinging to her like a heavy cloak.

"Mirella?" Riven's voice cut through the fog in her mind, and she looked up to find him standing beside her, his face full of concern. He reached for her, his fingers brushing her arm, grounding her back to reality. "Are you all right?"

She nodded, though her breath was still uneven. "I saw... I saw something." She looked up at him, the vision of the Night King still lingering in the back of her mind. "I saw you. And the darkness. The Night King. He's... he's coming for us."

Riven's expression darkened, and he stepped closer, his hand tightening around her wrist. "The Night King isn't just a shadow, Mirella. He is the curse. He's been tied to my bloodline for centuries, waiting for the moment when we would be strong enough to face him. And now, with you... with the bond we share..." His voice trailed off, as if he couldn't finish the thought.

Mirella felt the weight of his words settle over her, like a heavy stone sinking into her chest. They weren't just fighting the darkness. They were bound to it—tied to it in ways they couldn't escape.

She closed her eyes for a moment, trying to steady her breath, trying to shake the feeling of the shadow that had risen from the earth in her vision. But even with her eyes closed, the sense of unease remained, a dark pull in the pit of her stomach.

"We need to leave," she said, her voice shaking. "We need to keep moving. The Night King is coming. He's close."

But as she turned to look back toward the edge of the clearing, a figure emerged from the trees—tall, cloaked in dark robes, and with a presence so powerful that it seemed to ripple through the air like a wave.

Mirella's heart stopped.

Riven stepped in front of her immediately, his sword drawn in one fluid motion, his body tense. The figure's face was obscured by a hood, but the air around it shimmered with an unmistakable darkness. The figure's eyes glowed a dull red, and its mouth curled into a grin that sent a chill through Mirella's very soul.

"Riven," the figure said, its voice smooth and cold, like ice scraping against metal. "You've come far. Too far. It's time to end this."

Mirella's breath caught in her throat. The figure's voice—there was something familiar about it. But before she could say anything, the figure raised a hand, and the shadows around them seemed to deepen, growing heavier, suffocating.

"Who are you?" Riven demanded, his voice sharp with anger and caution. "What do you want?"

The figure's lips curled into a malicious smile, and it stepped forward, its eyes never leaving Riven. "I am Aric. And I have come to deliver a message—one that you will wish you had never received."

Mirella's heart thudded in her chest, and she took a step back, her mind spinning. Aric. Riven's former mentor. The name hung in the air like a death sentence, and Mirella could feel the weight of it pressing against her.

Riven's face went pale, and for the first time since they'd met, Mirella saw something resembling fear in his eyes. "Aric… You shouldn't have come."

The figure, Aric, tilted his head slightly, his smile widening. "But I had to, Riven. You and your little *companion* have been meddling in things far beyond your understanding. The prophecy is not a game. The bond you share with her… it's dangerous. And you are both *too* close to the truth."

Mirella's head spun with the implications of his words. She could feel Riven's tension radiating off him, his sword still poised, but there was something in his expression now—a cold, distant resignation.

"What do you mean, 'too close'?" she asked, her voice trembling with uncertainty. "What truth? What is this bond?"

Aric's eyes glinted with a knowing cruelty, and he stepped closer. "The truth, my dear, is that Riven's bloodline is cursed— not just because of the Night King's influence, but because the bond you share with him is a part of *the curse*. The prophecy isn't just about defeating the darkness—it's about *becoming* the darkness. And you, Mirella, are the key to it all."

Riven's hand tightened on the hilt of his sword. His eyes were filled with a storm of conflicting emotions—rage, fear, guilt. "No. You don't understand. I've spent my whole life trying to protect her from this."

Aric chuckled softly, the sound dark and foreboding.

Aric's laughter echoed through the clearing, a chilling sound that sent ripples of unease through Mirella's chest. The shadows around them seemed to grow thicker, darker, twisting into shapes that barely resembled the trees or the earth beneath their feet. The air itself seemed to shimmer with dark magic, the pressure of it pressing against her skin.

"You think you've protected her?" Aric's voice dripped with disdain. He took another step forward, his cloak swirling with the movement. "You've been doing exactly the opposite, Riven. By drawing her into this cursed bond, you've damned her to a fate she cannot escape."

Mirella felt her breath catch in her throat, the weight of his words crashing over her like a wave. She glanced at Riven, searching for any hint of the man she had come to trust, but his face was a mask of tension, his grip on his sword unyielding.

"Stop," Riven's voice was hoarse, barely a whisper, but it carried the weight of someone on the edge of breaking. He raised his sword in a defensive stance. "This is a lie, Aric. The prophecy—this curse—*it's* not her fault. It's my bloodline. It's mine to bear."

Mirella's mind raced, her heart thundering in her chest. What was Riven not telling her? The pieces of the puzzle were starting to come together, but the truth felt like a distant thing, just out of reach. The Night King, the bond, the curse—all of it twisted around them like a tightening noose.

"And yet, you've dragged her into it willingly," Aric spat, his eyes flashing with a cold, bitter rage. "The bond between you is *dangerous*, Riven. It isn't just fate. It's a binding of power, of *darkness*. The two of you—together—you will become the very thing that destroys this world."

Mirella's stomach churned as Aric's words sank in. She took a step back, her mind whirling. The forest around them pulsed with dark energy, the shadows feeling closer, as though the trees themselves were closing in, watching her. Every part of her body screamed to run, but something kept her rooted to the spot. Was it fear, or something deeper? Was it the bond Aric spoke of?

Riven's eyes flickered with a fleeting sadness before hardening again. "*You* don't get it, Aric. I'm not going to let her face this alone. I *can't*."

Aric's lips curled into a cruel smile. "You never had a choice, Riven. And neither does she. The darkness has claimed you both."

Mirella's legs felt unsteady, her body trembling with the weight of the tension in the air. Her eyes flicked from Aric to Riven, but all she could see was the storm that seemed to be rising between them. They were caught in something bigger than both of them, a curse that had already begun to tear them apart. Her breath came quicker, and she stepped toward Riven, not sure what she was trying to say, but desperate to break the silence that was suffocating her.

"Riven," she whispered, her voice shaking. "What does he mean? What is this bond? Is it really... *that* dangerous?"

Riven didn't look at her right away. His eyes were still locked on Aric, but there was a flicker of guilt there—a glimmer of something she couldn't fully understand. "Mirella..." His voice faltered, and for the first time since she'd met him, she saw the cracks in his armor. "The curse isn't just about me. It's about us. *Together*."

Her heart stopped, the words reverberating through her chest like an echo. "What does that mean?" she asked, her voice barely above a whisper, but there was a desperation in it that even she couldn't ignore.

Before he could answer, Aric stepped forward, his eyes narrowing in a look of contempt. "He won't tell you the whole truth, Mirella. He's too afraid of losing you to admit it. But I will."

Mirella's breath caught in her throat as Aric's gaze shifted to her. The shadows around him seemed to swirl more fiercely now, a dark energy emanating from his very being.

"The curse was forged centuries ago, a pact between Riven's bloodline and the Night King," Aric continued, his voice cold and final. "The prophecy spoke of two souls, bound together by the curse, fated to either destroy the Night King's shadow or become part of it. But the price for such a bond is always high. The darkness calls to them, and *in the end*, it will consume them both."

"Shut up, Aric," Riven growled, his sword now raised higher, the blade gleaming in the faint light of the Silver Tree. His muscles were tense, his body poised for action, but Mirella could see it in his eyes—he was holding back. And the words that Aric had spoken had shaken him, too.

Mirella looked at Riven, searching his face for answers, but he turned away, his jaw clenched so tightly it seemed as though he were forcing the words back.

But Aric wasn't finished.

"You think you can fight it, Riven?" Aric sneered. "You've always been able to outrun the truth, but you can't outrun the darkness inside of you. Not anymore. *You* are the key. And so is she."

Mirella's heart pounded in her chest. The weight of Aric's words pressed down on her like a vice, squeezing the air from her lungs. "What are you talking about?" she gasped, her eyes flicking between the two men, desperately trying to piece together the fragmented truth.

Aric's lips twisted into a smile. "The curse binds the two of you. Your souls, your fates. You are the Night King's true heirs. And when the time comes, the bond will be complete. It will either destroy you, or you will become the Night King's shadow. His queen."

The word *queen* hung in the air like a dagger. Mirella recoiled, her hands trembling at her sides, her mind reeling from the implications of what Aric had just said. Was that what the mark on her skin meant? Was she to become a part of this cursed legacy? Was she destined to be tied to the very darkness that had haunted Riven's bloodline for centuries?

"No," she whispered, the word slipping from her lips before she could stop it. "I won't. I won't become that. I can't."

Riven turned to face her, his eyes filled with regret and something else—something darker. "Mirella..." His voice was barely audible, like a whisper lost in the wind. "I never wanted this for you."

But it was too late. The shadows were already closing in, swirling around them with a force that pulled them both toward the darkness. Mirella could feel it—feel the weight of her bloodline, the curse, the magic, all pressing down on her, pulling at her heart.

Aric smiled, his gaze gleaming with cruel satisfaction. "It's too late to run now. The choice has been made."

The ground beneath them trembled, and a dark wind swept through the clearing, making the branches of the Silver Tree sway violently. A distant howl echoed from deep within the forest, followed by the sound of something crashing through the underbrush.

Mirella turned sharply, her heart racing. Something was

coming.

Riven's grip on his sword tightened. His eyes were fierce, burning with a mixture of resolve and fear. "Mirella," he said, his voice low and urgent, "we have to leave. Now."

She nodded, panic rising in her chest as the darkness began to press closer, as if the world itself was folding in on them. But she couldn't help it—she looked back at Riven, her heart caught in the storm of confusion and fear. *Could she trust him? Could she trust the bond they shared?*

Riven's eyes were filled with something that mirrored her own fear, but there was something else there too—something unspoken, a promise wrapped in pain.

They turned and ran, their footsteps heavy in the thickening shadows. The sound of pursuit grew louder, the howl growing closer, but no matter how fast they moved, the darkness was always just behind them.

And the Silver Tree, with all its ancient magic, loomed behind them—silent, watching, as the prophecy that had begun to unfold threatened to tear them apart.

Six

The Betrayal of the Heart

The moon hung low in the sky, its silvery glow casting long shadows across the forest as Riven and Mirella stumbled through the thick underbrush. Their breaths were ragged, their hearts beating as one in the chaotic silence that had taken hold between them. The Darkwoods had become a maze of twisted trees, their gnarled roots rising like serpents beneath their feet. The path ahead was unclear, but Riven's steady pace never faltered. Mirella, however, couldn't shake the unease in her chest, the nagging feeling that they were running toward something far darker than they could see.

Riven had remained silent since they fled from the Silver Tree, his eyes narrowed and distant, as though lost in thoughts too painful to share. Mirella could feel the tension between them, a palpable force that seemed to stretch the very air between them. She had tried to speak, tried to bridge the growing gap, but each time her words faltered under the weight of their situation.

What had Aric meant? The prophecy, the curse—Mirella's heart ached as she recalled the dark truths Aric had revealed. Riven's bloodline, tied to the Night King, the very darkness they had been fighting, and now… now Riven had been asked to choose: to embrace his shadow heritage or to sever his bond with her to save her from the same fate.

But how could she trust anything now? Was their love truly theirs, or was it another part of the curse? Had it been nothing more than manipulation from the very beginning? How much of Riven's feelings were tied to the bond, to the prophecy, and how much was truly him?

The thought gnawed at her, bitter and cold. She had believed in them. She had believed in the connection between them, the magnetic pull that had drawn them together from the first moment. But now, doubts clouded her mind, and she wasn't sure where the line between love and fate had blurred.

"Riven," she whispered, almost afraid to break the silence that had settled so heavily between them. "Why didn't you tell me?"

His body stiffened, and for the first time in what felt like an eternity, he glanced at her. His expression was unreadable, his eyes dark and heavy, as though the weight of the world had settled upon him.

"I didn't want you to know," he muttered, his voice thick with regret. "I thought I could protect you from this. From *him*."

The mention of the Night King sent a shiver down Mirella's spine. She clenched her fists, her nails digging into her palms. "So, you were just going to hide it from me? Everything? The curse, your bloodline... all of it?"

Riven stopped in his tracks, turning to face her. His chest rose and fell with each breath, his features etched with pain. "I didn't want you to carry the weight of it. The burden of my past, Mirella, is not something you should have to bear."

The words hit her like a slap. She wanted to scream at him, to demand answers for the betrayal that had lodged itself deep in her heart. But she didn't. She couldn't. Instead, she pressed her hand to her chest, trying to steady her breathing, trying to quell the rising tide of anger and hurt.

"Your past, your bloodline... It's a part of you," she said quietly, her voice trembling. "I can't just pretend it doesn't exist, Riven. I'm part of this now too, whether you like it or not."

Riven's jaw clenched, his eyes narrowing in frustration. "I know. But that doesn't change the fact that I'm cursed. That my blood is tied to the Night King's darkness. The bond between us... it's more than just love, Mirella. It's part of this twisted legacy."

Mirella felt the truth of his words crash over her like a wave. The connection between them, the bond that had felt so natural, so right, was not just fate—it was something darker, something more dangerous. The realization left a bitter taste in her mouth.

"And what does that mean?" she asked, her voice breaking slightly. "What does that mean for us, Riven? For *me*?"

Riven closed his eyes for a moment, as if the weight of the question pained him more than anything. "It means I have to make a choice. A choice I never wanted to face." He opened his eyes, and for the first time, Mirella saw the raw pain that lurked beneath his mask of stoicism. "I can embrace my bloodline. I can take my place by the Night King's side, and the darkness will consume us both. Or…" His voice trailed off, his gaze turning toward the ground as if he could not bear to meet her eyes.

"Or?" Mirella pressed, though she was afraid to hear the answer.

"Or I sever the bond," he said quietly, almost as if the words physically hurt him. "I can choose to save you from this curse, from the shadows that want to take you. I can walk away from you, Mirella, so that the darkness doesn't claim us both."

Mirella's heart shattered at his words. The very thought of losing him—of him turning away, of severing the bond between them—felt like a knife twisting in her chest. But beneath the heartbreak, there was something else, something far more painful.

"Why are you telling me this now?" she whispered, her eyes filling with tears she hadn't realized were there. "Why didn't you just… leave me? If this is the only way, then why not just go?"

The pain in his eyes deepened, and he took a step forward, his hand reaching out toward her, but she took a step back, unable to meet him halfway. "Because I can't," he said softly, his voice rough. "I can't leave you, Mirella. I don't want to. But I… I have to protect you. I *can't* let the darkness take you too."

The words were like a poison, and Mirella's chest tightened as her emotions warred within her. He was willing to sacrifice everything—their love, their bond, their future—just to protect her. And yet, in that sacrifice, he was asking her to let go. To let him go.

Riven was trapped in the weight of his lineage, the legacy of the curse, and his need to protect her. And in that struggle, he was pushing her away.

Mirella closed her eyes, fighting the overwhelming rush of emotions. She had thought their love could conquer anything. But now, she wasn't so sure. Was it all doomed from the start? Had she been swept up in something far beyond her control? Was she just another piece in the Night King's game?

She didn't know.

"I can't lose you," she whispered, her voice barely audible. "I can't lose what we have."

Riven stepped back, his eyes shadowed with pain. "If I stay… I'm only going to drag you deeper into the darkness. You have no idea what this will cost you."

"I don't care about the cost," she replied, her voice breaking. "I love you, Riven. *I trust you.*"

The words seemed to hang in the air, a desperate plea for him to understand. But instead of the relief she had hoped for, a terrible stillness settled over them both.

"You shouldn't," Riven whispered, his voice barely audible, as though saying it aloud caused something inside him to crack. "You *can't.*"

Mirella stared at him, her chest aching, the chasm between them widening with every passing second. The man she had trusted, the man she had fallen in love with, was being torn apart by the weight of his legacy. And in that moment, she saw it—*the darkness* that had claimed his soul long before she had met him.

Riven turned away, his back to her, his voice trembling with something between rage and despair. "I'll leave you, Mirella. I *have to.*"

She stepped forward, her heart screaming for him to turn back, but her feet were rooted to the ground. She couldn't move.

"Mirella, listen to me," he said, his words jagged. "You don't know what this will do to you. To us. If we stay together, if I continue to stand by your side, I'm *bringing* you into this curse. And when it takes hold, when the shadows come for us both, I won't be able to protect you. *I can't watch you fall too.*"

Mirella reached out, her hand trembling as she tried to close the gap between them, but the space felt insurmountable now, a canyon of pain and doubt that neither of them could cross.

"I don't care," she said fiercely, her voice breaking as she stepped closer to him. "I don't care if it hurts. I'll face the darkness with you, Riven. I'll face everything, because I love you."

But the words seemed to fall flat. Riven was already pulling away from her, the distance between them growing as he turned his face to the shadows, his shoulders shaking as if he couldn't bear to look at her.

The darkness was closing in, and Mirella realized, with an overwhelming sense of dread, that it wasn't just the curse that threatened to tear them apart. It was their own fears—their own betrayals, unspoken and raw.

Riven was leaving.

And she didn't know if she could stop him.

The forest around them seemed to close in, and for the first time, Mirella realized that the battle they faced wasn't just against the Night King.

It was a battle for their very souls.

Riven's footsteps echoed in the silence, heavy and determined as he turned his back to Mirella. The distance between them grew with each step he took, the space stretching out like an invisible gulf that threatened to swallow them both whole. Mirella stood frozen in the darkness, her heart aching with each movement he made away from her. She wanted to scream, to call him back, but her voice was trapped in her chest, a silent scream that no words could escape.

She felt the weight of his decision, the crushing reality that he had made up his mind. His sacrifice. His love for her, twisted and complicated by the curse that was bound to his bloodline. She had never imagined this—had never thought she would face the very real possibility of losing him, not because of some distant, looming threat, but because of the deep-rooted darkness inside him. The very thing he had tried to protect her from.

"Riven, please," her voice cracked, the words barely escaping her lips. She hadn't meant to say them out loud, but there they were, desperate and raw. "Don't leave me. I *can't*—"

But he didn't turn around. He kept walking, his silhouette swallowed by the dark trees ahead, as if the shadows themselves were pulling him into their embrace. Mirella felt like she was being torn apart, piece by piece, with each step he took away from her. Her chest felt hollow, the space inside her aching as if something vital had been ripped away. The forest, once so full of life and mystery, now felt like a prison.

"Riven!" she shouted, the words louder this time, filled with the raw desperation of a heart breaking under the weight of the curse. Her feet moved before her mind could catch up, the desire to stop him, to make him understand, propelling her forward.

But no matter how fast she ran, no matter how much her heart screamed for him to hear her, the distance between them grew.

He stopped suddenly, his back still to her, his shoulders stiff with some unseen tension. The forest was unnervingly quiet, the usual rustle of leaves and chirping of insects stilled by the tension that clung to the air. Mirella stopped just a few feet away from him, gasping for breath, her body trembling from the effort of chasing him down.

Riven turned slowly, his face cold and unreadable. The sadness in his eyes was overwhelming, but it was buried beneath a mask of determination that made her feel like he was already lost to her.

"Mirella," he said, his voice rough, filled with a sadness she had never heard from him before. "You don't understand. This is the only way. If I stay with you, the darkness will consume both of us. It's not just me anymore, it's you too."

His words hit her like a physical blow. The bond between them—the one they had fought for, the love they had built— was now a trap, a noose tightening around them both, and Riven was pushing her away to save her.

"You're wrong," Mirella whispered, her voice breaking. "You don't have to go. We can face this together. You *don't* have to choose between me and your bloodline. We can fight it. We *can* fight the curse."

Tears sprang to her eyes as she reached out toward him, but he took a step back, his gaze hardening.

"I wish I could believe that, Mirella," Riven's voice was tinged with regret, and he looked away as though he couldn't bear to meet her eyes. "But I've lived with this curse my whole life. I've seen what it does to people. To families. To the ones I love. You don't know what you're asking for."

"But I do," she said, her heart pounding in her chest. "I know you, Riven. I know your heart. I know you're more than your bloodline, more than the curse inside you. *I love you.* And I'm not afraid of this. Of *us.* Please," she begged, her voice pleading as she stepped closer, "Don't leave me."

Riven's face softened for a moment, the pain in his eyes almost unbearable. He opened his mouth as though to speak, but the words didn't come. Instead, he closed his eyes, his shoulders sagging with the weight of his internal battle.

"I have to leave," he said finally, his voice barely above a whisper. "I can't bear to watch you suffer because of me. I can't let the curse destroy what we have."

With that, he turned and began to walk again, his steps quicker this time, as if he couldn't bear to be near her any longer. Mirella felt her heart crack with each of his steps, and before she knew it, she was moving, running after him, her feet pounding against the earth beneath her.

"Riven, stop!" she cried, her voice desperate, the words coming from the deepest part of her heart. "Please. I won't let you do this. *We* won't let you do this!"

But he didn't stop. He couldn't. The pain in his eyes told her everything she needed to know. He had already made his decision.

Mirella's legs burned from the effort of chasing him, but she refused to give up. She couldn't. She wouldn't let the darkness, or the curse, or Riven's past, tear them apart. She wasn't going to lose him—not like this.

Suddenly, a violent shift in the air made her freeze. The trees above them seemed to tremble, and the ground rumbled with a low, foreboding growl. The forest itself seemed to be reacting to the storm brewing inside them. Shadows crept closer, stretching out as though alive, wrapping themselves around the trees, and the moonlight—once so comforting—

was swallowed by an unnatural darkness.

Mirella turned, her heart pounding, and felt it then—the pulse of magic that swept through the forest like an unstoppable wave. The air crackled with dark energy, heavy with the promise of something ancient and malevolent. It wasn't just the curse at work anymore—it was the Night King. His presence was like a suffocating blanket, pressing in on her, on Riven.

"No," Riven's voice was hoarse, a rasp of fear in his chest. "It's too late."

He pulled Mirella back, his hand gripping her arm tightly, but she fought him, pushing him away. The shadows were closing in, their tendrils creeping through the clearing, reaching for them, swallowing the light around them. She could hear the whispers now—the hissing of dark voices, voices that came from the very shadows themselves.

But it wasn't just the shadows that had come for them.

In the distance, a figure emerged from the blackness. Tall, cloaked in darkness, with eyes glowing an unnatural red. The figure moved with a terrifying speed, a blur of shadows, its form shifting and rippling like liquid darkness.

The Night King.

Riven's grip on her tightened, and for the first time, Mirella saw true fear in his eyes.

"We have to go. Now," Riven said, his voice tight with urgency. "The darkness is here. The choice has been made for us. Run!"

But Mirella couldn't move. She couldn't leave him. Not now. Not like this.

"Riven—no. We *fight* together," she said, her voice trembling but resolute.

He turned to her then, and for a brief, unbearable moment, their eyes locked. She saw the pain in his gaze, the battle within him, the sorrow. And she saw something else—the love he still felt for her, the love he wanted to protect.

But then, he turned away.

"I'm sorry," he whispered, so softly that she almost didn't hear him.

Before she could react, Riven pushed her back into the trees, the force of it knocking her to the ground. He turned, sword raised, and with a defiant cry, he met the darkness head-on, his blade cutting through the shadows that leaped at him with terrifying speed.

Mirella scrambled to her feet, her heart pounding with every beat, as the forest seemed to close in around them. The shadows were everywhere, suffocating her, trying to pull her under. She could feel the Night King's presence, dark and cold, seeping into her very soul.

Riven was fighting, but she knew—*he couldn't win alone.*

With a desperate cry, Mirella reached deep within herself, pulling on the magic that had once felt foreign, now a part of her, a force that surged within her veins. She reached for the sigil on her chest, her fingers brushing the mark that burned against her skin, and she cried out to the darkness.

"No! *Not him!*"

In that instant, the world around her shifted. The shadows recoiled, the air crackled with magic, and the darkness that had been closing in suddenly faltered.

But it wasn't enough.

Riven's sword clashed against the Night King's shadows, and Mirella's heart screamed as the force of the battle seemed to shake the earth beneath her.

"Riven!" she cried, her voice hoarse, desperate.

The answer she received was not what she had expected.

The shadows closed in, the darkness swallowing him whole.

And then, all that remained was the echo of his name.

Seven

The Call of the Moon

Mirella's feet felt heavy as she walked alone, the winding path up the Moonspire growing steeper with each step. The air around her was thick with a chill that had nothing to do with the temperature. It was as if the mountain itself had come alive, pulling at her with every movement, urging her to move forward, deeper into its embrace.

The Moonspire was not a place for the faint of heart. Legends spoke of the mountain as a sacred site, a place where the moon's power was at its peak, where the veil between worlds thinned and the ancient magic of the land surged like a river. For years, people had made pilgrimages to this mountain, seeking answers, but few had ever returned. And those who did spoke of strange occurrences—visions, whispers, and a call from the moon that none could fully understand.

Mirella had heard the whispers of the moon herself. For

days, she had felt it pulling at her, urging her to leave the safety of the camp where she had taken refuge after the chaos of the last few days. The curse, Riven's decision to distance himself from her, the darkness growing stronger with each passing day—it was too much to bear. She could feel herself unraveling, the weight of the prophecy, the bond, and the curse pulling her in every direction.

But the Moonspire… It was her only chance.

Her only hope.

With each step up the rocky trail, the air grew thinner, the moonlight stronger. By now, it was almost as if the mountain itself was shifting beneath her feet, guiding her toward the summit. The silver light bathed everything in an eerie glow, casting long shadows that seemed to move of their own accord. The trees around her twisted unnaturally, their branches bending as though reaching for her, their forms barely visible in the mist.

She had never been this far up the mountain, never this close to the source of the power. And yet, as she drew nearer to the peak, the connection to the shadows within her deepened. She could feel the magic stirring inside her, winding through her like smoke, cold and dark. The sigil that had burned on her chest since the moment she had bonded with Riven pulsed faintly beneath her skin, a constant reminder of the curse that tied her to him.

But this was different. The air, the earth, the very mountain beneath her feet—all of it thrummed with power. It felt ancient, unyielding, as if the answers to everything she sought were just beyond her reach. She had to get to the summit. She had to know what the prophecy meant, what she was supposed to do.

Her breath grew more labored as she neared the top. The stone beneath her feet was slick with dew, and the wind had grown colder, biting into her skin. But she didn't stop. She couldn't.

The peak of the Moonspire was nothing like what she had imagined. A stone altar sat at its center, surrounded by a ring of ancient, weathered stones, each one carved with symbols too intricate to decipher. The altar glowed softly, as though the very stone itself was alive, infused with the power of the moon. The light seemed to radiate from it, bathing the entire summit in a silver glow that made Mirella's heart race with anticipation.

As she stepped closer to the altar, the air around her seemed to hum with energy, the ground trembling beneath her feet as though the mountain itself was awakening. The moon above her shone brighter than ever, casting a silvery veil over the world.

Then, she heard it—a voice, soft but clear, whispering in the air, its words almost too faint to catch.

Come closer, Mirella.

The voice was familiar—unnervingly so—but she couldn't place it. It was both soothing and terrifying, as if it were calling to something deep within her. She paused, her heart hammering in her chest. The voice beckoned to her, coaxing her forward.

Embrace what you are. Embrace the shadows. You are the key to the world's salvation.

The words settled deep within her, but they also filled her with a strange, creeping fear. She had always known that the darkness had a power within it, something that had been bound to her bloodline for generations. But this… this felt different.

The shadows weren't just part of the curse now—they were inside her, in her very soul.

Mirella's hand trembled as she reached out toward the altar. The sigil on her chest burned hotter, and the shadows around her deepened, pulling closer as if they could sense her hesitation. Her breath caught in her throat as she touched the stone. A shock of power shot through her, a pulse of cold energy that sank into her very core, leaving her dizzy and disoriented.

You've come so far, Mirella. Now you must decide. The voice was clearer now, resonating deep within her chest. *The shadows within you are not a curse. They are power. Power you were born to wield. All you must do is accept it.*

Mirella's mind raced, her thoughts tangled in a web of fear, doubt, and longing. The voice was right in some ways. The power—the dark magic—was inside her, undeniable, growing with each passing day. She had felt it for so long, ever since she first touched the Silver Tree, ever since the sigil had appeared on her skin. But could she truly embrace it? Could she accept the darkness, the very thing that had caused Riven so much pain?

The answer was within her. She knew it. Deep inside, she knew what she had to do. The moon's power, the shadows—everything had led her here, to this moment, to this choice.

But the pull of Riven's memory, of their love, was just as strong. Could she really abandon him? Could she choose to embrace the very thing that threatened to tear them apart?

Riven... she thought, her heart heavy with sorrow. The man she loved, the man she had been bound to by the curse. Could she sever that bond to save him? To save herself?

The shadows seemed to grow thicker around her, wrapping

themselves around her like a cloak. She could feel their power, their temptation, calling to her, urging her to give in. It was so easy, so seductive. The darkness wasn't evil—it was simply *power.* Power she could control, power that could change everything.

Come, Mirella. The voice called again, urging her forward. *Accept your true nature. Embrace the shadows. Only then will you be free.*

A part of her wanted to. A part of her ached for the release, for the answers, for the strength that lay in accepting the shadows fully. She could feel the darkness within her, restless and waiting, its power just beyond her reach. It could be hers. She could wield it. The power to end the curse, to save the world, to bring balance to the forces that had torn her life apart.

But at what cost?

She closed her eyes, feeling the weight of the decision settle on her shoulders. Could she face the truth of what the shadows were asking of her? Could she truly become what the voice in her head was urging her to be? A queen of darkness, wielding the power of the Night King's legacy? Or would she risk everything—her connection to the shadows, her very soul—to save Riven, to protect him, and to stay true to the love that had once felt pure?

Her heart ached. The love for Riven, the love that had bound them together from the very beginning, was the one thing that had kept her grounded. The one thing that kept her from falling into the abyss of darkness.

But what if I can have both?

Her thoughts were fragmented, desperate. She wasn't ready to give up on their love—not yet. But she wasn't sure she could ignore the power growing inside her either.

A gust of wind stirred the air around her, the moonlight flickering like a dying star. The shadows swirled around her, tightening, pressing closer, until she could feel them clawing at her skin. And then, in a sudden moment of clarity, she knew.

This was her choice to make. And whatever she chose, there would be no turning back.

The voice seemed to grow stronger, the shadows pulling her closer, and for a moment, the darkness overwhelmed her senses, drowning out all rational thought.

She took a deep breath.

Then, with trembling hands, she placed both of her palms flat on the altar.

A burst of cold, silver light filled the air, blinding her, and the shadows rushed in. The sigil on her chest flared with a painful intensity, burning brighter than ever before, and the power surged through her. The moon's light enveloped her like a second skin, wrapping around her as the darkness coiled tighter inside her, filling her veins with its power.

And in that moment, she knew that the shadows were no longer something to fear. They were part of her—her inheritance, her strength, and the very thing that could save them all.

But at what cost?

As the last of the light dimmed, the moon above her seemed to gaze down, cold and unblinking, watching as Mirella stood between the light and the shadows, her choice now made.

She was no longer just a girl bound by fate.

She was the one who would shape it.

And with that, the Moonspire fell silent, its ancient secrets unraveling before her.

The silver light from the moon shimmered across the mountaintop, illuminating the altar where Mirella stood, her hands still pressed against the ancient stone. The power that coursed through her veins was unlike anything she had ever felt before—cold as winter's breath, yet intoxicating in its intensity. It surged through her like an untamed river, carving new paths within her, binding her to something far greater than herself.

For a moment, she couldn't breathe.

The shadows coiled around her ankles, whispering in voices too many to count. They weren't menacing, not like the darkness she had fought before. No, this was something different—something ancient, something *alive*. It wasn't just darkness. It was knowledge. A power long forgotten, waiting for someone to claim it.

This is who you are, the voice whispered again, softer now, weaving into the very air around her. *This is what you were always meant to be.*

Mirella gasped, her vision flickering as the world shifted around her. Images flooded her mind—fragmented and dreamlike, yet so vivid she could *feel* them.

A woman stood beneath a blood-red moon, her silver hair streaming behind her, eyes dark as the void. She held her arms out, commanding the shadows to rise around her, and the earth trembled beneath her power.

Then another vision—this time of a man, standing at the edge of a battlefield, his sword dripping with black ichor. His face was hidden in shadow, but his presence was undeniable. Power radiated from him, and in his hand, he held a silver pendant, glowing with the same sigil that burned against Mirella's skin.

And then—pain.

A sharp, unbearable pain that tore through her chest, forcing her to her knees. She gasped, clutching at her mark as it burned brighter, the heat searing into her flesh. The visions collapsed around her, and suddenly, she was back on the Moonspire, the night air thick with silence.

Her breaths came in ragged, uneven bursts. The power inside her was still humming, alive and potent, and the shadows around her seemed to shift in response. She *felt* them. Not as enemies, not as invaders—but as part of her.

Mirella clenched her fists, steadying herself. She wasn't the same girl who had begun this journey. The darkness, the prophecy, the curse—she could no longer separate herself from them.

And yet, in the depths of her soul, there was still something that tethered her to the light. Something that refused to break, no matter how deeply the shadows tried to claim her.

Riven.

She closed her eyes, reaching for the bond that still pulsed faintly between them, even after everything. The magic that had linked them was weak, strained, but it was still *there*. She could feel him—somewhere far away, lost in the void of shadows, fighting against something unseen.

Was he calling for her?

Or was he slipping further into the darkness?

A cold gust of wind rushed over the mountain, and suddenly, she felt *it*. A presence.

Someone was watching her.

Mirella's eyes snapped open, and she spun around, her pulse hammering in her ears. The mountaintop was empty, save for the silver altar and the endless night beyond. But she *felt* it—a pair of eyes in the dark, something lurking just beyond the veil of shadows.

Then, from the mist, a figure stepped forward.

A man, tall and composed, his presence exuding an eerie calm. His hair was the color of midnight, his features sharp and aristocratic, as if he had been carved from the very shadows themselves. His eyes—dark, bottomless—studied her with an intensity that made her skin prickle.

Mirella's breath hitched. She knew who he was before he even spoke.

The Night King.

He was more than just a figure of legend, more than a whispered warning. He was real. And he was standing before her, his presence so strong that the very air around him seemed to bend to his will.

A slow, knowing smile curved his lips as he stepped closer.

"You've finally heard the call," he murmured, his voice smooth as silk yet laced with something ancient, something predatory. "I was beginning to wonder how long you would resist."

Mirella forced herself to stand tall, even as her heart pounded wildly in her chest. "I didn't come here for *you*," she said, her voice steady despite the storm raging inside her. "I came for answers."

The Night King tilted his head slightly, amused. "And yet, here I am. The answer you seek." His gaze flicked to the sigil on her chest, glowing faintly beneath her clothes. "You feel it, don't you? The power within you. The bond that ties you to the darkness."

Mirella clenched her fists. "The bond that ties me to *Riven*," she corrected.

The Night King chuckled, a low, almost condescending sound. "Ah, yes. The boy who has spent his entire life running from what he is. I suppose it's only natural you still cling to him. But tell me, Mirella—do you truly believe he will return to you? That he will *choose* you, knowing what he must become to stand against me?"

Mirella's chest ached at his words, but she refused to let them shake her. "I don't need to *believe* in him. I *know* him."

The Night King sighed as if mildly disappointed. "A shame. I had hoped you were ready to accept the truth." He took another step closer, and the air around them darkened, the shadows reaching for him like loyal subjects. "You are stronger than he ever was, Mirella. And deep down, you know it."

Mirella's jaw tightened. "If I am so strong, then why are you trying so hard to sway me?"

A flicker of amusement crossed his features, but there was something else lurking beneath it—something unreadable. "Because I *see* you," he said softly, his voice carrying an undeniable weight. "I see the fire within you, the power that yearns to be free. And I see the chains you have wrapped around yourself, the way you fight against what you are."

Mirella exhaled sharply, forcing herself to stand her ground. "And what exactly do you think I *am*?"

The Night King's smile widened. "You are the missing half of the prophecy. The one who will tip the scales. You are my queen."

Mirella's heart nearly stopped.

The words crashed into her like a tidal wave, sending her mind reeling. "You're lying," she said, shaking her head. "You're trying to manipulate me."

"Am I?" The Night King's gaze never wavered, his presence pressing against her like an inescapable force. "You feel it, don't you? The darkness within you. The way it calls to me."

She *did* feel it. It was undeniable—the power in her veins, the whispers of the shadows, the way the Night King's presence resonated with something deep inside her. She had been fighting it for so long, afraid of what it meant.

But what if embracing it didn't mean losing herself?

What if the only way to save Riven, to end the curse, was to *accept* the power instead of running from it?

The Night King extended his hand toward her, palm open, inviting. "Come with me, Mirella. Together, we will reshape the world. You were never meant to stand beside Riven. *You were meant to stand beside me.*"

The wind howled around them, the silver light of the moon casting long shadows across the mountaintop. Mirella's heart pounded as she stared at his outstretched hand, torn between the power within her and the love she refused to abandon.

The choice was hers.

The darkness waited.

And the world would never be the same.

Eight

Love's Sacrifice

The wind howled as Mirella descended the Moonspire, her mind a storm of uncertainty. The Night King's words lingered, curling around her thoughts like smoke. *You were meant to stand beside me.* The darkness had beckoned her, whispered of power, of purpose. And for the briefest moment, she had felt it—*understood* it.

But she had turned away.

The cold mountain air bit into her skin, but she barely noticed. There was only one thought in her mind now. *Riven.*

She had to find him.

She had to bring him back.

The journey back to where she had last seen him was a blur. Time had become meaningless, the landscape shifting in her periphery as if the very world around her had begun to fold inward. The deeper into the forest she ran, the more the shadows seemed to reach for her, slithering along the ground like living things. But she wasn't afraid.

Not anymore.

Her heart knew where to find him.

The moment she stepped into the clearing, she felt the shift. The air was thicker, heavier, charged with an unnatural force. The sky above was shrouded in restless clouds, the moon barely visible through the swirling darkness.

And then she saw him.

Riven stood at the edge of the clearing, his back to her, his head bowed. Shadows clung to him like a second skin, curling around his limbs, seeping from his very being. The silver sigil that had once connected them glowed faintly on his chest, but it was different now—warped, darker, as though something had tainted it from within.

Her breath caught.

"Riven," she whispered.

He tensed at the sound of her voice but didn't turn.

Mirella took a cautious step forward. "I looked for you. I—I thought I lost you."

His shoulders rose and fell with a deep breath. When he finally turned to face her, her stomach clenched. His eyes— once filled with fire and determination—were different now. A storm raged within them, something deep and broken, something *changed*. The pull between them was stronger than before, but there was something else, something foreign, as though the shadows had taken root inside him.

"Mirella," he murmured, his voice raw.

She stepped closer, reaching for him, but he flinched away, his hands clenched into fists at his sides.

"I shouldn't have come back," he said, his voice barely above a whisper.

Her heart clenched. "Don't say that."

"I'm not who I was," he said, his jaw tight. "I *feel* it, Mirella. The darkness. The bloodline. I can't fight it anymore."

She shook her head fiercely. "Yes, you can. You *are* fighting it."

"No." His voice was firm now, and when he looked at her, the pain in his eyes was unbearable. "You don't understand. I let it in."

Silence stretched between them, heavy and suffocating.

Mirella forced herself to breathe. "What does that mean?"

Riven exhaled sharply, raking a hand through his dark hair. "The Night King's power… it's in me now. I stopped fighting it. I thought I could control it, but it's changing me." His fists clenched tighter. "And if I stay with you, Mirella, if this bond remains, I will *destroy* you."

She felt the words like a physical blow, but she didn't waver. "I don't believe that."

"You should," he said, stepping back. "Because I do."

The agony in his voice sent shivers through her, but she refused to let fear take hold. She wouldn't lose him. Not like this.

The sigil on her chest flared suddenly, a heat that coursed through her veins. The bond between them—it was still alive, pulsing with energy, fighting against whatever darkness threatened to pull him away.

She moved without thinking, crossing the space between them. Before he could stop her, she reached up and pressed her palm against his chest, against the sigil that connected them.

A shock of energy erupted between them, a force so powerful that the very ground trembled beneath their feet. Riven gasped, his hand flying to her wrist, as though to pull her away, but he *didn't.* His grip tightened instead, his breath unsteady.

Their magic clashed, intertwined—light and dark, fire and shadow.

"Mirella," he choked out, his fingers curling around her arm.

"I'm not afraid," she said fiercely, her voice steady despite the storm raging around them. "I won't let you lose yourself to this."

His expression twisted with something between desperation and longing. "You don't understand—"

A sudden, deafening *crack* split the air, and the world around them seemed to *shudder.*

Mirella barely had time to react before the shadows coalesced at the edge of the clearing, forming into a shape—tall, monstrous, eyes gleaming like burning embers.

A guardian of the Night King.

Its presence sent a pulse of dread through her.

The creature's voice was a whisper and a roar all at once, a sound that sent ice through her veins.

"He belongs to us now."

Mirella's breath caught. She stepped in front of Riven instinctively, her magic flaring to life, the sigil on her chest burning bright.

"You're wrong," she said, voice steady despite the terror curling inside her.

The creature tilted its head, amused. "You cannot save what is already lost."

Riven stepped forward then, his own shadows rising around him. But Mirella could *feel* the conflict in him, the war raging in his heart. He was slipping. The darkness had its claws in him, and it was dragging him deeper.

No.

She wouldn't let it.

With a deep breath, Mirella turned toward him. "Riven," she said, her voice low but unwavering. "Listen to me. We *fight* this. Together."

His eyes flickered, pain warring with something deeper.

But the creature let out a low, guttural laugh. "He cannot be saved."

Mirella clenched her fists. "Watch me."

The creature lunged, its form twisting into a mass of shadows, surging toward them with unnatural speed.

Mirella didn't hesitate. She reached inside herself, grasping the power that had awakened in her atop the Moonspire. The light and the dark. The moon and the shadow.

With a cry, she released it.

The blast of silver energy exploded outward, colliding with the shadowy creature. The force of it sent a shockwave through the clearing, shattering the darkness like glass.

Riven gasped, staggering back as if pulled from a trance. His hand flew to his chest, to the sigil that still pulsed between them.

The creature let out an ear-piercing screech as its form was obliterated, dissolving into nothing.

Silence fell.

The air was thick, humming with the remnants of power. Mirella turned back to Riven, breathless, her body trembling from the force of the magic she had just unleashed.

Riven was staring at her, wide-eyed, his expression unreadable. "Mirella..."

She stepped closer. "I won't lose you," she whispered.

For the first time since she had returned, something in Riven's face *broke*. The war within him wasn't over, but she had given him a choice—given him a reason to *fight*.

Slowly, hesitantly, he reached for her. His fingers brushed against her cheek, and in that touch, she felt everything—his pain, his longing, his love.

He hadn't been lost. Not yet.

And as long as she had breath in her lungs, she would fight to keep it that way.

Even if it meant sacrificing everything.

The air still hummed with the echoes of the battle, but the clearing around them was once again cloaked in an eerie stillness. Mirella's heart pounded in her chest as she stood face to face with Riven, the weight of everything that had just transpired settling around them like a thick fog.

His fingers brushed against her cheek, his touch tentative, as if he were afraid she might disappear if he held on too tightly. Her breath caught, the raw vulnerability in his eyes almost too much to bear. He was still fighting it—still torn between the shadows that had already begun to claim him and the love that was pulling him back toward her.

Mirella reached out, cupping his face in her hands, feeling the warmth of his skin against hers. "Riven," she whispered, her voice barely audible. "You don't have to fight alone. I'm here. We can do this together."

For a moment, he didn't speak. His gaze dropped to the ground, and Mirella could see the conflict in the way his shoulders tensed, his muscles coiling like a man ready to run, ready to pull away. But the shadows around him were quieter now, less forceful, as if they, too, were waiting for him to make a decision.

"Mirella, I…" He swallowed hard, his voice trembling with a

pain that nearly broke her. "I want to believe that. But I don't know how to *not* be this."

Her heart clenched. "You are not just the darkness inside you, Riven. You are so much more. You are *us*. You are the man I love. And no matter how strong the shadows are, they can't take that from us."

His eyes flickered, his gaze uncertain, torn between the love they shared and the undeniable force pulling him toward his shadow heritage. "I can feel it," he said softly, his voice breaking. "The shadows are growing stronger, and every time I resist, they pull harder. I'm afraid that if I stay with you, Mirella, I'll lose myself. I'll lose *us*."

The pain in his voice was a dagger through her heart. But she wouldn't let him pull away. She couldn't. Not when they had fought so hard to be together.

"No," she whispered fiercely, her hands tightening on his face, forcing him to look at her. "You won't lose us. You can't. You don't have to give in to the darkness. We can fight it—together. We've already faced so much. We can face this, too."

Riven's eyes softened with an emotion she couldn't quite name. A flicker of hope? A quiet surrender? She couldn't tell, but in that moment, he seemed to soften. The shadows around him retreated, just a fraction, as though they, too, were hesitating.

The tension between them was unbearable. Mirella could feel the storm raging in his chest, the magic—both light and dark—clashing violently inside him. But she wasn't afraid. Not anymore.

"I love you," she said, her voice steady with certainty. "I'm not asking you to change. I'm asking you to *choose*."

Riven's gaze locked with hers, and for the first time since

they'd come together on this cursed path, she saw something else in his eyes. A flicker of understanding. The deep, overwhelming love they shared, tempered with the reality of the curse, was more than he had ever believed it could be. And for that moment, he allowed himself to believe it.

"I choose you," he whispered, the words raw with emotion.

It was as if the entire world shifted. The air around them lightened, the oppressive weight of the curse easing just slightly. Mirella pulled him close, her hands gripping the back of his neck as she kissed him—gentle, but full of everything she had wanted to say. Everything she had wanted to feel. In his arms, the world felt right again, even if just for a moment.

When they finally pulled apart, their foreheads touched, and they stood there in the quiet aftermath of the battle, the weight of the decision they had made hanging between them.

But that peace was fleeting.

The ground beneath their feet rumbled again, more violently this time. Mirella's heart dropped as the earth shook, sending a tremor through her limbs. She pulled away from Riven instinctively, her eyes scanning the shadows that had begun to stir once more.

"No," she murmured, her chest tightening with dread. "It's not over."

Riven's face hardened with resolve. "It never is."

Before they could react, the air grew colder, the shadows darker. From the depths of the forest came a figure—a dark silhouette, taller than a man, a shape more like a wraith than anything human. It was cloaked in the very shadows themselves, its eyes glowing with an unholy light. As it stepped into the clearing, the air seemed to thicken, and the very fabric of the world felt stretched and fragile.

The Night King had arrived.

Mirella's heart raced as she stepped back, her pulse quickening at the sight of the monster that had haunted her dreams, the very embodiment of everything she feared. But this time, there was no fear. There was only determination.

"You," the Night King said, his voice like the wind itself—cold, distant, and full of ancient power. "You think you can resist me? You, who bear my legacy?"

Mirella stood her ground, feeling the magic stir within her, the power of the moon and the shadows alive in her blood. She had made her choice. She wasn't afraid anymore. Not of him, not of the darkness.

The Night King's eyes narrowed as he regarded her. "You think you have a choice in all of this? You think you can save him?"

Riven stepped forward, standing beside her. "We're not afraid of you," he said, his voice firm, his stance strong. "We've chosen each other, and nothing you do can change that."

The Night King's laugh was chilling, echoing through the clearing like a death knell. "You *are* afraid. And you will be again, when you realize what you've chosen. You are bound to me, whether you accept it or not."

Mirella felt the pull of his words, the cold chill that threatened to wrap itself around her heart. But she wasn't alone anymore. Riven's hand found hers, and she squeezed it, grounding herself in their connection.

"We will never belong to you," Mirella said, her voice rising with each word, her magic flaring. "We are *not* your pawns."

The Night King's gaze darkened, and in an instant, he surged forward, his hands outstretched. Shadows curled around his fingertips like snakes, and the very ground beneath their feet seemed to crack and splinter as he unleashed his power.

Riven stepped in front of her, raising his sword in a defensive stance, but Mirella didn't hesitate. She reached deep within herself, pulling on the power she had embraced—the light and the dark that now coursed through her veins.

The battle had begun.

The clearing was filled with a blinding flash of light as Mirella released her magic, the force of it pushing back the shadows, forcing the Night King to stagger. His eyes burned with rage, but Mirella felt the surge of power within her, both terrifying and exhilarating.

Riven's sword clashed with the Night King's dark magic, the shockwave of their battle sending tremors through the earth. Mirella could feel Riven's struggle, the weight of his curse, but he was fighting. For her. For them.

The darkness around them seemed to grow, feeding off their fear, their doubts. But Mirella didn't let it take hold. She had chosen. She had *chosen* him, and she would fight for them both, even if it meant sacrificing everything.

"Riven!" she called, her voice cutting through the chaos. "We can do this. We can end this together!"

And in that moment, as the moon's light flared above them, they fought side by side, determined to face the darkness—no matter the cost.

Nine

Into the Abyss

The path leading into the Abyss was no path at all—just a twisted descent into a darkness so deep that even the moonlight seemed to falter at its edge. Mirella felt it, the very air around her thick with the pulse of ancient magic. The earth beneath her feet was slick, blackened, and foreign, the soil almost alive with the remnants of an old, forgotten power. The trees that lined the way were gnarled and twisted, their skeletal branches clawing at the air like the fingers of long-dead giants.

Mirella's breath was shallow, the weight of the journey pressing heavily on her chest. Every step deeper into the Abyss seemed to steal more of the light, the very moon above her growing dimmer as though it, too, was being consumed by the darkness below. She could feel it—the ancient, terrible force that had awaited them for centuries. The Night King was near, his shadow stretching across the land, his presence like a constant, gnawing ache in her bones.

But it wasn't just the Night King that she feared.

It was *Riven.*

She glanced at him, her heart aching at the sight of him beside her. The bond that had once burned brightly between them had become strained, distant, almost painfully fragile. His eyes—those familiar, once-fiery eyes—were hollow now, shadowed with a growing darkness that threatened to pull him away from her. His once proud, unyielding stance had become slumped, weighed down by the curse that had settled deep inside him.

The shadows, once only an occasional companion, now clung to him like a second skin, swirling around his body with every movement. She could feel the pull of it, the way they *called* to him, their whispers beckoning him toward the Night King's throne, toward his legacy—toward his *destiny.*

She wanted to reach out, to pull him back into the light, but the weight of his struggle was too great. Mirella couldn't deny it: the battle raging inside Riven was no longer just his own—it was hers, too. They were tethered together, bound by fate, by love, by the darkness itself.

"Riven..." she said, her voice breaking the oppressive silence. She hadn't said his name like that in days, hadn't allowed herself to. It felt too much like a plea, a reminder of all the things they could lose.

Riven didn't answer right away. His eyes were fixed ahead, his jaw clenched. The shadows around him thickened, swirling in unnatural patterns, like a storm on the verge of breaking. His lips parted, but the words that came were strained, almost strangled.

"I can feel it, Mirella." His voice was hoarse, raw with

something she couldn't name. "It's calling to me. The shadows… they want me. And I don't know how much longer I can fight it."

Her heart lurched, and she reached for him, her fingers trembling as they brushed against his arm. "You can fight it, Riven. You've always fought it. Don't let it take you."

His gaze flickered to her, his eyes clouded with regret and pain. "I'm not sure I can anymore. I'm *losing* myself."

"No," she said firmly, her voice cutting through the thick silence. "You are *not* losing yourself. You're still the man I love. And I won't let you fall into this darkness."

Riven's hand moved to his chest, pressing against the sigil that still burned faintly beneath his clothing. The shadows seemed to gather tighter around him, and the air grew colder, heavier. "You don't understand," he whispered, his voice breaking. "The Night King's legacy… it's in me. It's always been in me. I've been fighting it my entire life. But now… now it's too strong."

Mirella could see the torment in his eyes, the conflict that was slowly consuming him. The more he resisted, the stronger the pull became. The shadows were winning, and there was nothing she could do to stop it. Not alone.

They reached the edge of the Abyss then, and Mirella stopped, her heart sinking at the sight before them.

The chasm stretched wide, a vast, yawning rift in the world itself. The air above the abyss shimmered with an unnatural haze, like heat rising from an open flame, but there was no warmth. Only cold. The shadows gathered here, swirling and coiling in thick masses, as if the Abyss itself was alive— breathing, waiting. The ground beneath their feet was cracked, jagged, as though the very earth was about to split open, swallowing them whole.

Mirella's gaze moved upward, where a pale light glimmered faintly in the distance—the Night King's throne, seated high atop a craggy spire of stone, casting a sickly glow on the abyssal void below.

A chill ran down her spine as the air grew heavier. The Night King was near.

"Riven…" she whispered again, her voice trembling. "This is it. The place where everything ends. *Where you choose.*"

Riven turned to her, his face pale, his eyes distant. "I don't have a choice," he said, his voice empty, resigned. "The darkness has already claimed me."

"No," Mirella said fiercely, her voice rising with renewed determination. "It hasn't. You're still you. I believe in you, Riven. I believe in us. And if we go into the Abyss, we go together."

But even as the words left her lips, the shadows around them seemed to thicken, pressing in on them from every direction. A soft whisper tickled the edges of her mind, a voice she had heard once before.

Come, Mirella. Come into the shadows. Come and claim what is yours.

It was the same voice that had spoken to her at the Moon-spire, urging her to embrace the darkness. She could feel it now, deep in her bones—the pull of the shadows, the weight of her inheritance, the power that surged within her. The moonlight was fading, and in its place, the cold embrace of the darkness beckoned.

Riven…

The moment of truth had come.

Mirella closed her eyes, forcing herself to breathe, to calm the storm that had begun to rise within her. She had made her choice before. She had chosen *love*, chosen *Riven*, and she would choose him again. She had to.

Riven's eyes met hers, and for the briefest moment, something passed between them—a flicker of understanding, of recognition, of the love that still burned despite the shadows that sought to snuff it out.

"Mirella," he whispered, his voice hoarse. "You shouldn't have come here. It's too dangerous."

She shook her head. "I don't care about danger. I care about you."

Riven's hand reached out to touch hers, the warmth of his touch grounding her amidst the cold that had threatened to swallow them. He looked down at their hands, his fingers tracing over the sigil on her skin.

"You don't understand," he said again, his voice filled with regret. "The shadows… they're inside me, Mirella. They want to consume me. They're *changing* me."

But Mirella didn't back away. She stepped closer, her heart resolute. "Then I'll fight them with you. We're stronger together, Riven. I won't let you go. Not to the darkness. Not to him."

She could see the storm inside him, the battle between light and shadow, love and darkness. And for a moment, she saw a flicker of hope, a glimmer of the man she loved, the one who had stood by her side when the world seemed to be falling apart.

"I won't let you become the Night King's puppet," she whispered, her voice filled with fierce determination. "Not while I'm here."

But even as she said the words, she could feel it—the abyss

was closing in. The shadows pulsed with a hunger she couldn't ignore. The pull of the Night King was *strong*, relentless. And Riven was slipping.

The ground beneath them trembled again, and the shadows surged forward, rushing toward them like a flood. Mirella barely had time to react before Riven staggered back, the shadows around him thickening, swirling with unnatural force.

"Mirella…" His voice cracked with pain. "I can't… I can't stop them."

She reached for him, her heart breaking, but the shadows pushed her away, swirling violently between them, growing thicker, darker.

"Riven!" she cried, her voice rising above the chaos.

And then, without warning, the shadows began to pull him toward the Abyss, toward the Night King's throne, his body jerking against the force of their pull.

Mirella's heart leaped into her throat. She couldn't let him go—*not like this.*

With every ounce of her strength, she reached deep within herself, pulling on the magic that had once felt so foreign, now a part of her very being. She felt the power surge through her—moonlight and shadow, light and dark, intertwined—and with a fierce cry, she summoned it all. The magic exploded from her in a wave of silver and shadow, shoving the darkness back with the force of a storm.

The shadows screamed, recoiling, but the pull on Riven was stronger. Mirella's hands reached for him, and the sigil on her chest flared bright, brighter than ever before, the connection between them crackling with energy.

"Riven!" she shouted, her voice hoarse with desperation.

"Come back to me!"

And then, as if the very heavens had answered, Riven's eyes met hers—finally. For the first time in days, the darkness lifted from his gaze, and in that fleeting moment, Mirella saw the man she loved.

With a final, defiant scream, Riven broke free from the shadows' grasp, stumbling toward her.

But the fight wasn't over. The abyss still yawned before them, the Night King's call echoing in the depths.

And now, with their connection more powerful than ever, Mirella and Riven had to make their final stand.

The shadows still had their claws in him.

But together, they would fight. Together, they would face the abyss. Together, they would choose *light*—even if it meant sacrificing everything.

Riven's eyes locked onto Mirella's as the last of the shadows recoiled from him, their grip loosening just enough for him to step forward. But as his feet moved, the ground beneath them trembled, and a new presence descended from the abyss—the Night King.

He appeared as if born from the very darkness itself, his form shifting and flickering with unnatural energy. His cloak was a swirling mass of shadows, and his eyes glowed a fierce crimson that pierced through the thickening blackness like twin beacons. He was taller than any mortal man, his very presence warping the air, twisting the fabric of reality around him. The abyss seemed to answer his call, pulsating with a dark, malevolent energy that bled into the world.

The Night King's voice rang out, deep and resonant, as if the words were woven from the very fabric of night. "So, you resist.

You cling to the light, Mirella, Riven." He stepped forward, his steps causing the earth to crack and splinter. "But what you do not understand is this: *You were never meant to be free.*"

Mirella took a step forward, her heart pounding in her chest. The shadows continued to swirl at Riven's feet, as if trying to pull him back toward the abyss. But he didn't falter, his hand gripping hers with a quiet strength that gave her hope. They were together now, more than ever.

"I choose light, *not* darkness," Riven said, his voice steady despite the storm inside him. "I will *never* choose you, Night King."

The Night King's lips twisted into a grin, predatory and cruel. "You misunderstand. It is not a *choice* for you to make. You were born into this legacy, bound to it, and no matter how hard you fight, it will consume you."

Mirella's breath caught in her throat. His words were like poison, sinking deep into her heart. But she couldn't— *wouldn't*—let them take root. Not now, not when everything they had fought for was within their grasp. She would not allow herself to be part of the Night King's twisted plan, nor would she let Riven succumb to the fate he feared so much.

"No," she said, her voice shaking with a force she hadn't known she possessed. "You don't get to make the rules, Night King. We choose who we become."

Riven squeezed her hand tighter, his other hand rising, fingers trembling as they reached for the sigil on his chest. The bond between them flared to life, sparking with an energy that lit the shadows around them like a beacon. The sigil was alive again, pulsing with the power of their love, a force that the Night King could never understand.

The air crackled with magic. The very ground beneath them

quaked as the darkness began to lash out, wrapping around them like tendrils, trying to bind them, consume them.

Mirella reached out, her heart full of determination. "We won't let you win."

Her words were more than just a defiance; they were a vow. She drew on every ounce of power she had, every bit of magic that had awoken within her since the moment she touched the Silver Tree. Her power surged, igniting her veins with the energy of the moon, the shadows, and the love she held for Riven.

The Night King hissed in fury, raising his arms, his shadows twisting into monstrous shapes around him, lashing toward them. "You think your love can defeat me?" he mocked. "You cannot overcome the darkness. You are mine to command."

The shadows surged, encircling Mirella and Riven, threatening to tear them apart. Mirella felt the weight of the Night King's power bearing down on her, trying to crush her under its suffocating grip. The air was thick with magic, the very essence of the abyss pressing in from all sides. But she couldn't—wouldn't—give up.

With a desperate cry, she channeled all of her strength into the sigil on her chest, pulling on the magic she shared with Riven. The sigil flared brighter, burning with a fierce intensity, and in that moment, she felt the shadows recoil. She could feel the Night King's power weakening, his hold on them slipping as the magic they shared began to overpower his darkness.

Riven's voice joined hers, low and steady, as he reached deep within himself, his own power flaring to life. "Together," he whispered.

The bond between them flared, a blaze of silver and shadow, a force so powerful that it sent ripples of energy out in all directions. The shadows wavered, then recoiled, as though they were afraid of the light they had tried so desperately to extinguish.

The Night King staggered back, his eyes wide with disbelief. The force of their combined magic pushed against him like a wall, holding him back, forcing him to retreat into the darkness that had spawned him.

"You *will not* break us," Mirella said, her voice now a roaring cry, stronger than any fear the darkness could create. The words felt like an incantation, a declaration of their will to survive, to live and love despite the curse that had bound them from the very beginning.

With a final, desperate roar, the Night King reached toward them, his fingers elongating, his form bending and twisting as he tried to break through the barrier of light and shadow they had created together. But it was too late. Mirella and Riven, their bond unbreakable, had finally chosen. And the light of their love burned brighter than any darkness.

In a blinding flash, the Night King screamed as he was forced back into the Abyss, his form dissipating like smoke on the wind. The ground beneath their feet trembled once more, and the very air around them seemed to shift, the weight of the darkness lifting as the night began to break.

Mirella collapsed into Riven's arms, her chest heaving as the last of the shadows vanished into the depths of the Abyss. Her body shook with the remnants of the power they had unleashed, but the silence that followed was deafening. They were alive. They had won. But the cost of their victory still hung between them like a fragile thread.

Riven's breath was hot against her ear as he held her tightly, his heart still racing. "We did it," he murmured, his voice thick with disbelief. "We *did* it."

Mirella pulled back slightly to look up at him, her eyes filled with a mixture of relief and fear. The battle was over, but the war—*their* war—was far from won. The Night King was gone, but the curse that had bound them together still lingered.

"We did," she said softly. "But we're not done yet, Riven. The shadows haven't gone. And neither have we."

He looked down at her, and for the first time in what felt like an eternity, the shadows around him seemed to recede. His eyes, though still haunted by what he had been through, were filled with something else now—hope.

"Together," he whispered again, his lips brushing against hers.

And in that moment, Mirella knew that whatever trials lay ahead, whatever shadows would rise again, they would face them side by side. They had chosen each other. And together, they would choose love over darkness, no matter the cost.

The moon above them burned brighter than ever, its light finally breaking through the clouds as the dawn began to rise.

And in the light of the new day, the Abyss that had nearly consumed them seemed a distant memory.

But they both knew the truth. The darkness had not been defeated. Not yet.

It was only waiting for its next move.

But no matter how long they had to fight, no matter how hard the road would be, they would face it together. Their love, and the power it held, was stronger than anything the shadows could throw at them.

Together, they would endure.

Ten

The Night King's Throne

The air in the heart of the Abyss felt heavier than ever, thick with the dark magic that swirled around them. The moonlight was a faint memory now, lost in the suffocating shadows that twisted and coiled like living creatures. The ground beneath Mirella's feet had turned to black stone, jagged and unforgiving, a stark contrast to the softer soil they had walked before. The path ahead was lined with strange, ancient carvings that glowed faintly with a sickly green light—symbols too old to comprehend, too filled with malice to ignore.

Riven walked beside her, his once-proud stride now weighed down by the shadows that clung to him, curling around his limbs like a serpent's grip. His face was pale, drawn tight with the inner battle that had begun the moment they had set foot in this cursed place. Mirella could feel the pull of the shadows around him, could see how they sought to swallow him whole.

His every step, every breath, seemed like a battle between the man she loved and the darkness that threatened to consume him.

The Night King was waiting for them.

They had come so far, traversing the heart of the Abyss, and yet now, standing before the throne of the dark ruler, the very air seemed to hum with an unnatural energy. The throne itself loomed before them, a monstrous structure carved from black obsidian and jagged stone, sitting atop a high platform like a throne forged from nightmare. The air around it shimmered, rippling with the dark magic that seeped from it.

And then, they saw him.

The Night King sat upon his throne, his form an ominous silhouette against the swirling darkness of the Abyss. His cloak was a mass of swirling shadows, undulating and shifting with a life of its own. His eyes burned with an otherworldly fire, glowing a deep, blood-red as he regarded them with a look of pure disdain.

"Welcome," the Night King's voice echoed through the vast chamber, deep and cold, vibrating with power. It was a voice that carried the weight of ages, as though it had been carved into the very stones of the world. "I've been expecting you."

Mirella's heart beat faster as she and Riven stepped forward, their every footstep sounding hollow in the vast expanse of the chamber. The shadows seemed to follow them, pressing in from all sides as though the very walls of the Abyss were closing in.

The Night King's smile twisted, dark and cruel. "You've done well to come this far. Most would have fallen long ago."

Riven's hand instinctively reached for the sword at his side, but Mirella placed a gentle hand on his arm, stopping him. She could feel the weight of the decision in the air, could sense the growing tension between them.

"Why are we here?" Mirella demanded, her voice firm but laced with fear. "What do you want from us?"

The Night King's eyes flickered to her, and for a moment, there was something almost *tender* in his gaze, as if he were looking at a piece of art instead of a foe. "What I want is simple, Mirella," he said, his voice smooth and filled with honeyed malice. "I want what was promised. I want what is mine by right."

He stood from his throne, his presence filling the room like a storm. "You two," he continued, gesturing to her and Riven, "were always meant to come here. You were always meant to fulfill the prophecy. The bond between you was no accident— it was written long before you were born."

Mirella's stomach twisted with a sense of foreboding. The words he spoke were chilling, as though they had been predestined, as though she and Riven had been nothing more than pieces in a game they hadn't even realized they were playing.

"What do you mean?" she asked, her voice barely above a whisper, the weight of the truth beginning to settle upon her.

Riven stiffened beside her, his eyes never leaving the Night King, as though he were waiting for something—some sign— that the darkness hadn't claimed him entirely.

The Night King's smile grew wider, as if he enjoyed the tension. "You, Mirella, and you, Riven, were chosen long ago to either bring about an eternal night or restore balance to the world. Your bond—this *curse* that you believe you're trapped in—it is the key."

Mirella's heart stuttered in her chest. She had known, on some level, that they were bound by something beyond fate, beyond love. But hearing it, hearing the Night King speak of it so plainly, was enough to send a cold chill through her.

"I don't believe you," she said firmly, stepping forward. "This bond doesn't belong to you. It belongs to *us*. It's our choice."

The Night King chuckled darkly. "Ah, yes. The naive belief that love can conquer everything. *It* is your choice, that much is true. But what you fail to realize is that the choice has already been made. The bond you share is not just about love, it is about the balance of this world. And you, Mirella, are the final piece. The darkness in you has always been there, waiting. The shadows you feel—the ones you believe you must fight—*they are part of you*. You were born to wield them."

Riven's breath caught beside her, and Mirella felt his pulse quicken beneath her hand. His body tensed, his every muscle coiled in response to the Night King's words.

"I *won't* accept this," Mirella said, her voice trembling with fury. "I won't let you control us. You don't get to decide what we are."

"Do you hear her, Riven?" The Night King's voice dropped to a soft whisper, almost coaxing. "She doesn't even understand the depth of her own power. But you, you feel it, don't you? The pull of the shadows. The weight of your heritage. The strength you could have, if you would only *accept it*."

Riven's eyes flickered, his hand tightening around Mirella's. His gaze was filled with a turmoil that mirrored the dark clouds gathering within him. Mirella could feel it, too. The pull, the temptation to *embrace* what he was. To give in to the power that had always been within him.

But she couldn't let him go. Not like this. Not to the Night King's side.

"I won't lose you to this," she whispered, her heart aching.

She turned to him, her voice pleading. "Riven, *please*. Don't listen to him. We *can* choose together."

Riven didn't respond. He simply stood there, his gaze locked on the Night King, torn between the woman he loved and the shadows that were growing stronger inside him. Mirella could see the struggle in his eyes, the inner war he fought, and it was breaking her heart.

The Night King smiled as though he knew exactly what was happening. "You see, Riven, it doesn't matter what you choose. You were born for this, just as Mirella was born to be your counterpart. And in the end, the darkness will claim you both."

Riven stepped forward then, his shoulders taut, his eyes filled with an emotion that tore at Mirella's heart. "Mirella, I…" He stopped, his voice strangled with emotion. "I don't know how much longer I can fight this. I can feel it. It's getting harder to resist. The shadows are part of me, and if I stay, I will pull you into the darkness with me."

Mirella's breath caught in her throat. "No. You can't say that. We'll fight it together, Riven. I won't let you go."

But he didn't answer. His eyes, filled with a mix of love and agony, turned toward the Night King once more. The shadows around him surged, writhing as if they were alive, pulling at him, pulling him toward the throne.

"Riven, *no*," Mirella cried, her voice breaking. "You can't—"

But it was too late.

The Night King's power surged forward, a tidal wave of darkness crashing over Riven. His body shuddered under the weight of it, and for a moment, Mirella feared she would lose him. The shadows wrapped themselves around him, enveloping him, pulling him away from her.

And in that instant, she knew—*knew* that Riven was slipping.

The pull of his shadow heritage was too strong. His love for her, for them, was the only thing keeping him from being swallowed whole.

Mirella stepped forward, her hands outstretched, her body trembling with desperation. "Riven!" she cried, but her voice was drowned out by the roar of the Night King's magic. The darkness swirled around them like a storm, thick and suffocating.

Riven's face twisted with pain, his expression torn between the love he had for her and the darkness that was consuming him. His hands reached for her, but the shadows pushed him back, pulling him toward the throne, away from the light they had once shared.

"Riven!" Mirella cried again, her voice breaking with anguish.

But the Night King's power surged once more, and Riven's form was swallowed by the darkness.

The world fell silent.

Mirella stood in the center of the Abyss, her heart torn in two, her body trembling as she stared at the place where Riven had been. The shadows closed in around her like a prison.

And in that silence, the Night King's voice echoed through the chamber.

"*Now*," he said softly, his voice laced with a dark satisfaction. "The choice has been made."

Mirella could feel the abyss pressing in, could feel the shadows wrapping around her, threatening to pull her down into their cold embrace.

But even in the heart of the darkness, she knew one thing.

She would never give up on Riven.

Not now. Not ever.

Mirella stood frozen, her heart hammering in her chest as the shadows swirled around her. The Night King's words echoed in her ears, and her body trembled with a mixture of fear and defiance. Riven, the man she loved, had been swallowed by the darkness, and yet, even in the depths of the Abyss, she could still feel him. The bond between them, however strained and fractured, was still there, pulsating with an energy she couldn't ignore.

The Night King's presence pressed down on her, suffocating, relentless. His cold gaze studied her from across the chamber, the malicious satisfaction in his eyes flickering like flames. His hand, glowing with dark energy, gestured toward the shadows swirling around Riven's form, now barely visible in the depths of the throne room.

"You see, Mirella," the Night King spoke, his voice smooth, almost coaxing. "The choice was never yours to make. You were always meant to fall into this darkness. You, and Riven. Your bond was written long before either of you were born."

Mirella's body quaked with anger, her eyes narrowing as she glared at the figure before her. "No," she spat, her voice raw with desperation. "I won't let you take him. You *can't*."

The Night King chuckled darkly, stepping closer to the center of the room. The shadows that had claimed Riven shifted and pulsed, as though they were alive, dragging him further from her with each passing second. The very air seemed to twist with his dark power.

"You think you have a choice? You think your love for him will save him from what he is destined to be?" The Night King's smile widened, a cruel, knowing grin. "You are wrong. All of this—*his* fate, *your* fate—it was written by forces far older than your love. It is inevitable."

Mirella's breath hitched, her mind spinning. His words were like poison, crawling beneath her skin, making her question everything. But she couldn't—*she wouldn't*—let him win. The love she had for Riven, the bond that tied them together, was stronger than any darkness. It had to be.

Her eyes locked onto Riven's figure, still struggling against the suffocating shadows, his body wracked with pain. She could see the desperation in his movements, the fight in his eyes. He was still fighting. He hadn't given up.

And neither would she.

Without another word, Mirella stepped forward, ignoring the sharp pull of the darkness around her. She reached out with every ounce of power she had left, feeling the burn of it course through her veins—the magic of the moon, of the earth, of the very light that had once seemed so far away, now surged inside her. She felt it, deep in her soul, the undeniable connection that had always existed between her and Riven.

"Riven," she called, her voice trembling, but strong, filling the silence of the Abyss. "I will not lose you. Not now. Not ever."

The shadows recoiled, twisting violently as if they were alive, but Mirella stood her ground. The sigil on her chest burned brightly, its light flaring as if it were responding to her words, to her power. She could feel the darkness recoiling from her, a subtle shift in the air.

"Stop!" she commanded, her voice gaining strength. "I will not let you take him."

The Night King's amused expression faltered for a moment, but he quickly regained his composure. "You cannot stop this, Mirella. You cannot stop what is already in motion."

But Mirella didn't care. She had made her choice. She would

fight for Riven. She would fight for their love, no matter the cost.

Her hands began to glow with silver light, and the shadows recoiled, writhing in opposition, but the power of her magic grew stronger, fueled by the depth of her resolve. The air around her pulsed with energy, the power of the moon coursing through her like an unstoppable tide.

"Riven," she whispered, closing her eyes as she focused all her strength into the bond they shared, letting it guide her. "Come back to me."

And then, with a strength she didn't know she had, she released her magic in a burst of brilliant light. The shadows around her, the darkness that had been pulling Riven into the Abyss, screamed in agony as the silver energy from Mirella's hands surged into the air, pushing back against the pull of the Night King's power. The very air seemed to crackle with energy as the light fought the darkness with everything it had.

The Night King snarled in frustration, raising his hands to unleash more of his shadowy magic, but it was too late. The light from Mirella's magic collided with the darkness, tearing through it like a beam of pure sunlight slicing through a storm.

"Mirella!" Riven's voice broke through the haze of shadows, desperate, raw, and filled with fear. "Mirella, I can't—"

"Yes, you can," she cried out, her voice full of determination. "You *can.*"

And in that moment, everything changed.

The shadows around Riven faltered, their grip weakening. He gasped, his body jerking as the suffocating force that had been dragging him into the Abyss released its hold, just for a moment. His eyes locked onto hers, and for the briefest second, the darkness around him flickered, as though even it could sense the power of their bond.

Mirella's chest tightened with fear, but she held on, reaching out toward him with all of her love, her magic, and her heart. "Come back to me, Riven. *Please.*"

Riven's chest heaved, and the shadows around him seemed to waver and flicker, as though they were losing their power. His body began to convulse, his skin pale, his face twisted with the torment of his struggle. The battle within him was reaching its climax, and Mirella could feel it—she could feel the pull of the darkness trying to reclaim him.

But she wouldn't let go.

With a final, desperate cry, Riven's hands shot out toward her, and as their fingers touched, the very air seemed to shudder.

The sigil on Mirella's chest flared brightly, and the bond between them exploded in a flash of light, a brilliant burst of energy that shattered the suffocating darkness around them. Riven's body jerked violently, but then, as if responding to the magic they shared, the shadows around him dissipated, crumbling into nothing.

For a heartbeat, everything stood still.

And then, Riven collapsed into her arms, his body trembling with exhaustion, his breath ragged. Mirella held him tight, feeling his heartbeat slowly stabilize beneath her hands.

"You're back," she whispered, tears stinging her eyes. "You're here. You're safe."

Riven looked up at her, his eyes filled with a mixture of relief and sorrow. "I don't know how much longer I could've fought it," he murmured, his voice thick with emotion. "I don't know what would have happened if you hadn't pulled me back."

Mirella's heart swelled with love, but there was no time to dwell on their victory. The Night King was still standing before them, his expression twisted with fury.

"You think you have won?" he hissed, his eyes glowing with malevolent rage. "You have only delayed the inevitable. You think the bond you share can stop what has been set in motion? *You cannot defeat me.* I am the darkness that has existed since time began."

Mirella looked up at the Night King, her body still trembling with the remnants of the power they had just unleashed, but her voice was strong. "No, Night King," she said, her words clear and resolute. "We choose our fate. We choose *light* over dark."

The Night King's expression twisted into a snarl, but Mirella didn't flinch. She could feel the power of her love for Riven, the strength of the bond that had pulled them through the Abyss, and the magic they shared. They had fought to be together, and nothing—no darkness, no shadow—could tear them apart.

"You've lost," Riven said, his voice steady but filled with resolve. "The bond between us is stronger than you. We won't let you destroy us."

The Night King's rage reached a fever pitch, his dark magic crackling with energy. But Mirella and Riven, united in their love, stood together. The sigil on her chest burned brighter than ever before, a beacon of light in the heart of the Abyss. The darkness around them began to waver, losing its grip, and the Night King let out a furious roar as his power faltered.

With one final, defiant cry, the Night King's form began to crumble, his body dissolving into shadow and ash, his power dissipating like a fading nightmare.

The Abyss trembled. The air crackled with the last remnants of his dark magic, but slowly, it began to fade. The oppressive weight of the shadows lifted, and the ground beneath their feet seemed to settle. The light from the moon above broke through the darkness, its silver glow filling the space where the Night King's throne had stood.

Riven and Mirella, breathing heavily, stood together, their hands still clasped. The weight of what had just transpired began to sink in. They had done it. They had defeated the Night King, but more importantly, they had *chosen*—together. They had chosen to fight, to love, and to embrace their bond, no matter the cost.

But in that victory, they both knew something else: the battle wasn't over. The world still needed to be healed, and their journey was far from complete. But as they stood there, the moonlight breaking through the shadows, Mirella and Riven knew one thing for certain.

Together, they would face whatever came next.

And they would *never* let the darkness take them.

Eleven

The Shattering of the Heart

The wind howled through the trees, carrying with it an unnatural chill that made the very air feel like a warning. Mirella stood at the edge of the clearing, her heart pounding in her chest, the tension between her and Riven palpable. The ritual they had decided to perform—one that had been whispered about in the darkest corners of magic—was their last hope. It was their only chance to stop the Night King, to rid the world of the darkness that had claimed so much of Riven. But the price of the ritual was far higher than anything they could have imagined.

The sky above them was a swirling mass of gray clouds, the moon barely visible through the thick haze. The air was dense with magic, the kind of energy that made the hairs on the back of Mirella's neck stand on end. The ritual they were about to perform required a balance, a fusion of light and shadow. It demanded their complete trust in each other, in their bond.

But neither of them knew if they could survive it.

Riven stood beside her, his posture tense, his eyes flickering with an internal war. His shadows were restless, swirling around him in an unsettling dance. They tugged at him, whispering, calling him back to the darkness, as if the very magic within him was fighting against the purity of what they were about to do.

"Are you sure about this?" Riven's voice was low, almost a growl, his gaze never leaving the ritual circle they had drawn in the dirt, its edges glowing faintly with a dark energy.

Mirella turned to face him, her heart heavy with the weight of their choices. She could feel his pain, his struggle, in every fiber of her being. The bond between them—the one they had fought so hard to keep intact—was now a lifeline. It was the thread that tied them together, but it was also a tether to the very darkness that threatened to consume him.

"I'm sure," she said, her voice steady despite the chaos swirling within her. "We don't have a choice, Riven. If we don't do this—if we don't stop him—we lose everything."

Riven's eyes darkened, the shadows growing thicker around him, wrapping tighter around his body like chains. "And what if the price is too high? What if this ritual tears us apart? I can't lose you, Mirella."

Her heart ached at the rawness of his words. She reached out, her hand trembling as it brushed against his. The moment their skin touched, a flash of light flared between them—brief, but intense. It was a flicker of the power they could wield together, the strength of their bond, but it was fragile, fading almost as quickly as it appeared.

"I won't let that happen," Mirella whispered, her eyes meeting his, fierce with determination. "We're in this together, Riven.

Always."

He closed his eyes for a moment, exhaling a shaky breath as though he were bracing himself for something unbearable. When he opened them again, there was a sadness there, a resignation that broke Mirella's heart. "I don't know if I can survive it, Mirella. The darkness in me—it wants to consume you. I can feel it, and I—" He stopped himself, shaking his head. "I can't let it happen."

The words hung in the air between them, heavy with the weight of what was about to happen. Mirella took a step closer, placing her hand over his heart, where she could feel the rapid beat of his pulse. She could feel the shadows within him, clawing, pulling, desperate for release.

"I'll fight with you," she said softly, her voice filled with a quiet intensity. "We don't have to fight alone."

Riven's eyes softened, and for a moment, he seemed to forget the battle within him. But the moment passed as quickly as it had come. He looked down at their hands, his grip tightening around hers, and Mirella could feel the resistance building within him.

"This is it," he said, his voice tight with emotion. "Once we start this, there's no turning back."

Mirella nodded, squeezing his hand. She could feel the ritual beginning to pull at them, drawing them both into its grip. The very air seemed to shift around them, vibrating with a growing tension. The dark energy from the shadows around them began to push against the light of her magic, threatening to overwhelm her. But she stood firm, focusing on the connection between them—the bond that was their strength, their only hope.

Together, they stepped into the center of the ritual circle.

Mirella took a deep breath, closing her eyes as she summoned the power within her—the moon's light, the pure magic that had always been a part of her. She could feel it stirring in her chest, a warm, golden light that pushed against the shadows. Beside her, Riven's darkness rose, his shadows swirling around him in response, more violent, more restless. His magic crackled, the power within him resisting her light.

They joined their hands, and the magic surged.

At first, it was beautiful—the blending of light and shadow, the way their powers intertwined, filling the air with a pulse of raw, vibrant energy. It felt as though they were one, their magic flowing through each other, their bond stronger than ever. For a brief moment, it seemed as though the ritual was a success—an overwhelming force that could undo the Night King's hold on Riven, and on the world.

But then, something shifted.

Mirella gasped, feeling a sharp pain in her chest as the shadows within Riven began to *fight* against her magic. The darkness was stronger than she had anticipated, clawing at her with a savage ferocity, determined to tear them apart. She could feel Riven's pain—the agony of his own inner battle—as the shadows threatened to overwhelm him, to take him back.

"Riven!" Mirella cried, her voice breaking. She tried to tighten her grip on him, but the shadows were pulling them apart, pushing them farther from each other. The light within her was flickering, struggling to hold its ground against the tide of darkness that Riven was battling inside.

"I can't hold on," Riven gasped, his face twisted with pain. "Mirella, I *can't*."

The bond between them flared with an unbearable heat, and Mirella felt the overwhelming power of the darkness inside him. It was too much. The shadows, the pull of his heritage, the curse—it was threatening to consume him entirely.

"No, please," Mirella begged, her voice filled with desperation. She could feel the ritual unraveling, the magic beginning to tear at the seams of their connection. "Riven, don't give up. *Please.*"

But Riven's eyes, filled with agony, met hers, and in that moment, she knew what he was about to do.

"Mirella," he whispered, his voice breaking. "I love you. But if I don't do this… I'll lose you. The darkness will take you with me. I can't—*I can't* let it happen."

She shook her head violently, tears springing to her eyes. "No! Don't say that! We can—"

But before she could finish, Riven stepped back, breaking their connection. The energy from the ritual snapped, the world around them collapsing into a swirling vortex of light and shadow. Mirella cried out as the bond between them shattered, the pain of it burning through her chest like a dagger.

Riven fell to his knees, clutching his chest as if the very act of severing the bond was tearing him apart from the inside. The shadows around him writhed in agony, but the light in his eyes was gone, replaced by something darker—something that scared Mirella more than she cared to admit.

"No, Riven," she whispered, her voice hoarse, her heart breaking. She stumbled toward him, her legs unsteady as she reached out for him, but the shadows around him pushed her back, their touch cold and cruel.

"I'm sorry," Riven murmured, his voice full of pain and regret. "I had to do this… for you."

Mirella fell to her knees beside him, her heart shattering as she reached for him again. "You don't have to do this. Please,

Riven... *please don't leave me."*

But he wouldn't meet her eyes. The darkness had taken him. The shadows had claimed him, and the bond that had once held them together was now gone.

She could feel it—the absence of him, the emptiness where the bond had once thrummed with life. It was like a part of her soul had been ripped away, and she was left with nothing but the cold, cruel reality of his sacrifice.

Riven had severed the bond to save her. He had chosen to break his own heart, to destroy the very thing that had kept them alive. And now, as she looked at him, she realized something even more painful.

The Night King had won. The darkness had taken Riven from her. And now, Mirella was alone.

With a broken heart, she looked up at the Night King, who stood watching them from across the clearing, his eyes gleaming with dark satisfaction.

"You see?" he said softly, his voice echoing in the cold air. "It was always meant to be this way. The light cannot exist without the darkness, and you, Mirella, were never meant to save him."

Mirella's fists clenched, her tears falling freely now. She didn't care about the Night King. She didn't care about his words.

Riven had sacrificed everything. And in that sacrifice, she would find the strength to fight.

Even without him. Even in the darkness.

She would never give up. Not now. Not while the world still needed her.

And as she stood, trembling but resolute, she knew that this was only the beginning of the fight. The Night King's victory would be short-lived.

Because Mirella would find a way to bring Riven back. No matter the cost.

Even if it meant tearing the world apart.

And she would *never* stop fighting.

Mirella stood in the silent aftermath, her breath ragged, her heart torn in two. The weight of Riven's sacrifice pressed down on her like a thousand stones. His eyes—empty and distant now—stared at nothing, the shadows that had claimed him seeming to feed on his essence, his spirit. The bond between them, the tether that had once connected them so firmly, had been severed, leaving nothing but a gaping void in its place. Mirella could still feel the lingering echo of the magic they had shared, but it was faint now, like a memory fading with time.

The Night King's laughter echoed through the clearing, a low, chilling sound that made Mirella's skin crawl. "You see, Mirella," he sneered, stepping closer, his dark form oozing malevolence. "It was never meant to be. You could never save him. Not with love, not with power. The darkness *owns* him now. And it will own you, too, in time."

She didn't look at him. Her gaze remained fixed on Riven, her mind whirling, her heart in agony. She could hear the Night King's words, but they didn't matter. None of it mattered. She had lost Riven, but that didn't mean she would stop fighting.

She couldn't stop. Not now. Not when the world was on the edge of annihilation.

The magic of the Abyss pulsed through her, cold and dark, swirling around her body like a cloak. The shadows, though weaker without the Night King's command, still whispered, still clawed at her, eager to take hold. But Mirella's resolve was unwavering. She was done with the darkness. She would not let it claim her, not after everything she had fought for, not after the sacrifice Riven had made.

A sharp pang of pain cut through her chest as she took a step toward him, reaching out, her hand trembling as she brushed against Riven's cold skin. His body was stiff, the shadows still clinging to him, wrapping around him like chains that couldn't be broken. She tried to push them away, but it was like fighting against a tidal wave. The darkness was too strong.

But her heart—her heart still burned with love for him, even if it was a flicker now, dimmed by the sacrifice they had made. She could feel it, that flicker of hope, buried beneath the suffocating weight of the darkness. If she could just hold on to that, just enough—

"You think you can save him, Mirella?" The Night King's voice was sharp, cutting through her thoughts. "You are as foolish as he was, thinking your love could change anything."

His words were like daggers, each one aimed at the very core of her being. But Mirella didn't flinch. She stood tall, her hands shaking with the fury that bubbled up inside her, her heart thudding with a fire that refused to go out.

"I will save him," she said, her voice low but filled with an intensity that made the Night King falter for a moment. "I will find a way."

The Night King stepped forward, his form almost blending with the shadows that surrounded him, his eyes glowing with a cruel light. "You cannot fight what is already inside you. The darkness is part of you, just as it is part of him. You cannot escape your fate."

Mirella's breath caught as a sudden realization hit her. She felt the pull—the bond between them—still there, faint but undeniable. The shadows were *still* clinging to her, tugging at her with every passing second. She could feel them growing stronger, feeding off the grief and pain that swelled inside her.

No. She couldn't let that happen.

With every ounce of her will, she pushed against it, focusing on the light that had always been a part of her, the magic that connected her to the moon, to the earth, to everything that was pure. She called on that magic, forcing the darkness back, just as she had done so many times before. The shadows hissed and recoiled, but they didn't relent. They wanted her. They wanted to claim her, just as they had claimed Riven.

"Mirella," the Night King's voice softened, almost coaxing. "You were always meant to be mine. Don't fight it."

"No," she replied, the word fierce and unwavering. "I'm not yours. I never will be."

She turned away from him, her focus shifting back to Riven. The energy in the air had grown thicker, the pull of the shadows stronger. Mirella could feel the walls closing in on her, but she didn't stop. She couldn't stop. She reached out again, her hand trembling as she touched Riven's chest. The shadows flared violently, but she didn't let them push her away. She closed her eyes, focusing all her magic on the bond they had shared, on the love that had always connected them.

The sigil on her chest burned fiercely, hotter than it ever had before. The power surged through her, a flood of light that fought against the darkness like a tide crashing against rocks. She could feel Riven's presence, faint but growing stronger as she drew on their connection. His pulse—his heartbeat—was still there, a faint but steady rhythm beneath her fingers. He was still alive. He was still *there*.

"Riven," she whispered, her voice breaking with the weight

of everything that had happened. "Come back to me. Please."

The shadows around Riven writhed in response to her words, thrashing and twisting as if they, too, were fighting against her magic. She could feel the darkness pulling at her—threatening to tear her apart, to drag her into the Abyss with him—but she held on. She couldn't give up on him. She *wouldn't*.

"Riven," she repeated, her voice now a firm, unwavering command. "Fight this. *Fight with me.*"

For a long moment, there was nothing but silence.

And then—*a breath.*

It was faint, barely perceptible, but it was enough.

Riven's body twitched, a subtle movement, as though the shadows around him were losing their grip. The sigil on her chest burned brighter, pulsing with a steady rhythm, as though responding to Riven's heartbeat. The shadows recoiled again, but this time, they didn't return. They were weakening.

Mirella's heart soared with hope, but she knew the fight wasn't over. The Night King's influence was still there, still strong, but with Riven's power fighting alongside hers, they could win. She just had to reach him—*she had to.*

"Riven," she whispered again, louder this time. "You are not the darkness. You are not what you fear. You are *you*. Please, come back."

Riven's eyes flickered, his gaze struggling to focus as if the darkness within him were clouding his vision. But there was something in his eyes now, a glimmer of recognition, a flicker of life beneath the shadowed surface.

"I… I don't know if I can…" His voice was weak, strained, as though the very act of speaking was an immense effort.

Mirella took his hand in both of hers, feeling the warmth of it, the pulse beneath his skin. She refused to let him go. "You can, Riven. You *will*. I'm here. I'm not leaving you."

The shadows that had once clung to him now hesitated, retreating ever so slightly. Mirella felt it—the tug of Riven's spirit, fighting back against the darkness, clawing its way to the surface. She couldn't stop the tears that fell as she gazed into his eyes, the pain of everything they had been through, everything they had *lost*, rushing to the surface.

But she also couldn't stop the love that still burned inside her, the love that was stronger than anything the darkness could offer.

"I love you," she whispered, her voice raw. "I love you, Riven. Don't let the darkness take you."

And in that moment, as the moonlight began to filter through the cracks in the clouds above, Riven's eyes cleared, and he looked at her with the clarity she had been longing for. His hand tightened around hers.

"I won't," he whispered back, his voice filled with a quiet strength that made her heart swell. "I'll fight for you. For us."

The shadows began to dissipate, retreating from him like a nightmare fading at dawn. And for the first time in what felt like an eternity, the light that had once burned between them flared back to life, strong and unyielding.

Together, they had broken the curse.

Together, they had defeated the darkness.

But the battle was far from over.

The Night King was not done.

And the world—*their world*—was still hanging in the balance.

But for the first time in a long while, Mirella felt something she hadn't felt in days.

Hope.

Twelve

The Breaking of the Curse

The abyss trembled. Shadows recoiled like wounded beasts, hissing and writhing as the force of Mirella's magic pushed against the suffocating darkness. The Night King stood before her, unmoving, his form a swirling mass of black mist, his crimson eyes burning like dying embers. The final confrontation had begun.

Mirella's breath came in ragged gasps, her body battered and worn from the battle, but she would not—*could not*—fall now. Not when Riven was still trapped between the light and the darkness. Not when everything they had fought for hung in the balance. The magic inside her surged, a molten force of moonlight and power that she could barely contain.

She took a step forward. The Night King smiled.

"You are brave, Mirella," he said, his voice smooth as silk yet sharp as a dagger. "But bravery alone will not save you."

Mirella clenched her fists, ignoring the chill that seeped into her bones. "I don't need saving," she said, her voice steady. "Not from you."

A dark chuckle rumbled from his throat. "Ah, but you still don't see, do you? You and I are not so different. The power inside you—the darkness you refuse to acknowledge—it is part of you. It *is* you." He tilted his head, studying her with an almost amused curiosity. "You have fought for so long, tried so desperately to separate yourself from the shadow, from *me*. But you cannot change what you were *born* to be."

Mirella swallowed hard. The shadows stirred around her, whispering in voices she did not want to understand. She had felt it—the darkness inside her. She had ignored it, denied it, pushed it away at every turn. But deep down, had she always known the truth?

She lifted her gaze, meeting his eyes. "I am not *you*," she said, her voice firm.

The Night King sighed as if disappointed. "Perhaps not yet. But soon, you will see."

With a flick of his wrist, the shadows lurched forward like a tidal wave. They crashed against her, wrapping around her limbs, digging into her skin like icy claws. She gasped, staggering back as the darkness threatened to smother her. It seeped into her thoughts, into her heart, whispering of power, of control.

You don't have to be weak.

You don't have to suffer.

Embrace us, and you will never feel pain again.

Mirella squeezed her eyes shut, fighting against the pull. She could feel it—the temptation, the weight of the darkness pressing against her. And in that moment, she understood.

This wasn't just a battle against the Night King.

This was a battle against herself.

She opened her eyes. The sigil on her chest flared, and with a scream, she unleashed the power of the moon. Silver light erupted from her body, burning through the shadows, pushing them back. The darkness howled as it recoiled, retreating into the corners of the abyss.

The Night King narrowed his eyes. "So, you have chosen, then?"

Mirella's breath was unsteady, but her resolve did not waver. "I *was* born with darkness inside me," she admitted. "But that doesn't mean it owns me."

She raised her hands, and the light of the moon answered her call. The air around her shimmered as raw energy built within her chest, flooding through her veins like liquid fire. The power of the silver moon—the very force that had chosen her—was hers to command.

The Night King's form flickered, shifting and warping as the light bore down on him. "You are a fool, Mirella," he hissed, his voice now edged with rage. "Do you truly believe that you can break a curse woven by the gods themselves?"

Mirella's heart pounded as she took another step forward. "I don't *believe*—I *know*."

The power inside her burned brighter, brighter than it ever had before. The sigil on her chest pulsed, and for the first time, she saw the strands of magic that bound the curse—the invisible threads of fate that had trapped her and Riven in an endless cycle of suffering.

And she saw how to *break* them.

With a deep breath, she raised her hands, fingers trembling as she reached for the threads of magic entwined around her fate. The moment she touched them, agony lanced through her body. The curse *fought* her, resisting with everything it had. It did not want to be undone. It had existed for too long.

The Night King's eyes widened in realization. "*No!*"

The shadows surged forward, desperate to stop her, but Mirella stood firm. She gritted her teeth, pushing through the pain, pulling at the threads of the curse, unraveling them one by one.

The world around her shuddered. The abyss trembled. The shadows screamed.

And then—

A *snap*.

A sound like the breaking of a thousand chains echoed through the air.

The curse was undone.

The magic around her exploded outward in a shockwave of silver light, consuming everything in its path. The darkness shattered, the abyss trembled, and the Night King let out a scream of pure rage as his form began to disintegrate, the very essence of his existence crumbling beneath the weight of her magic.

Mirella fell to her knees, gasping for breath. The light around her flickered, then dimmed. The world was silent.

It was over.

The curse was broken.

But at what cost?

She turned, her heart clenching as she searched for Riven. He lay motionless on the ground, his body still and lifeless. The shadows that had once clung to him were gone, but so was the bond between them—the tether that had connected their souls.

"No," she whispered, crawling toward him. "No, no, no."

She reached for him, her hands shaking as she cupped his face. He was cold. Too cold.

"Riven, wake up," she begged, pressing her forehead to his. "Please."

Nothing.

Tears burned her eyes, spilling onto his skin as she shook him. "You promised," she choked out. "You promised me you'd fight."

Still, nothing.

The world blurred around her, the weight of her grief crushing her beneath it. She had broken the curse. She had won. But she had lost him.

A soft wind brushed against her skin.

And then—

A faint breath.

Mirella gasped, her hands stilling as she felt the rise and fall of Riven's chest. It was weak, fragile, but it was *there*.

Then, slowly, agonizingly, his fingers twitched. His lips parted, and a hoarse whisper escaped.

"Mirella…"

A sob tore from her throat as she pulled him into her arms, holding him tightly, feeling the warmth return to his skin. He was alive. *He was alive.*

Riven's hand weakly found hers, his grip barely there. "You… did it," he murmured, his voice rough.

Mirella let out a watery laugh, pressing a kiss to his forehead. "We did it."

The abyss around them was gone. The darkness had been vanquished. The sky above was no longer shrouded in eternal night.

The curse was broken.

And though the road ahead would not be easy, though the scars of what they had endured would never truly fade, they had each other.

And that was enough.

Mirella's hands trembled as she held Riven in her arms, her fingers brushing the sweat-drenched strands of his hair. His breaths were shallow, but they were steady now. His warmth, the pulse of life within him, was the most precious thing she had ever known. The weight of everything they had endured, the darkness, the fear, the pain—had been worth this moment. She felt the bond between them stir, faint but undeniable, a flicker of light in the midst of everything they had lost.

But as much as she wanted to bask in the relief of his return, the reality of their situation pressed down on her like a heavy cloak. The night was still long, and there was no telling what the consequences of breaking the curse would be. The world around them had been reshaped, remade by the very forces they had battled.

"Riven," she whispered, brushing her thumb across his jaw, feeling the roughness of his skin. His eyes fluttered open, his gaze unfocused at first, as though he were still fighting to surface from the depths of the shadows.

"Mirella," he rasped, his voice thick with exhaustion. "What happened? I... I don't remember..."

"You were consumed by the darkness," she said softly, her voice trembling with emotion. "The curse—it was inside you. I had to sever the bond. It was the only way to save you."

Riven's face twisted in pain, his brow furrowing as memories came rushing back. His hand moved to his chest, as if he could feel the echoes of the battle, the magic they had wielded, the bond that had once connected them. "I felt… everything slipping away. I thought—" He coughed, and Mirella's heart clenched at the vulnerability in his voice. "I thought I lost you. I thought… I was going to lose myself."

"You didn't," Mirella replied fiercely, leaning down to kiss his forehead gently. "You're here. You're with me."

But even as she said the words, doubt tugged at her heart. The curse had been broken, yes—but at what cost? Riven had severed their bond, choosing to protect her, to sacrifice his own connection to her to ensure she wasn't consumed by the darkness. The weight of that choice was more than she could bear.

"I don't know how to live without you," she admitted, her voice a soft whisper, as if the very air around them could steal away her words.

Riven reached up weakly, his fingers brushing against her face. His touch was so faint, but it still sent a shiver through her. "You don't have to," he said, his voice hoarse but filled with a gentle strength. "I'm here. I'm not going anywhere."

Mirella's chest tightened. She wanted to believe him, to feel the warmth of his promise in every fiber of her being. But she knew the truth: their connection had been severed. The bond that had kept them tethered together, no matter the darkness, was now gone. She had broken it to save him. But could she survive without it?

The world around them was still. The air, once thick with magic, now hung in a heavy silence, as though even nature was holding its breath, waiting for something to happen. Mirella looked around, her senses alert to every sound, every shift in the atmosphere. It was as if the ground beneath them was holding its breath, unsure of what was to come next.

"I can't stay here," Riven said suddenly, his voice more urgent now. His fingers gripped her arm with surprising strength. "We can't. The Night King—he's not gone. Not really. His influence is still here. In the earth. In the air. I can feel it, Mirella."

She shook her head. "We defeated him. The curse is broken. We're free."

Riven's gaze darkened. "No," he said, his voice grave. "We've broken the curse. But the Night King's power—his magic— it's more than just the curse. It's tied to the very fabric of this world. The darkness, Mirella, it's in the land itself. The balance is shifting."

Mirella's breath caught in her throat as the weight of his words settled over her. The darkness wasn't just a force that had controlled them, a power that had bound Riven and her together. It was something older. It was a presence that had seeped into the world itself, and no matter how much they fought, no matter how much they had given to break it, it would not simply vanish.

The moon above them, once a steady beacon of light, flickered, its silver glow dimming as if in response to the words. Mirella turned her eyes upward, watching as the stars seemed to tremble in the night sky, their light waning.

"Riven, what do we do?" she asked, her voice trembling with the uncertainty of their future. "How do we stop this? How do we save the world?"

Riven's hand fell to his side, and his body slumped, exhaustion settling in as he finally allowed himself to rest. "I don't know. But we have to *go*. We need to leave the Abyss. There are places where the darkness is weaker. Places where the curse can't reach. The only way to *contain* the Night King's magic is to destroy the source of it."

"The source?" Mirella repeated, her mind racing. "Where is it?"

Riven met her gaze with a look of grim determination. "The Night King's throne. The place where he drew his power from. We've taken his physical form, but the magic—the heart of it—is still there. We must destroy it. It's the only way to stop him from rising again."

Mirella swallowed, her throat tight. Her body ached from the ritual, from the magic, from everything they had endured to break the curse. But there was no time to rest. There was no time for the weight of their loss to sink in. The world they had fought to save still teetered on the brink of destruction, and if they didn't act now, it would all be lost.

The ruins of the Night King's throne lay ahead, towering above them like a dark sentinel. The obsidian spire, once a symbol of his power, now seemed to pulse with malevolent energy. The world felt wrong. There was no light here, no warmth. The shadows reached up from the earth, crawling toward them, eager to reclaim the darkness they had so desperately tried to banish.

Riven stood slowly, his strength returning as the magic in the air surged again. Mirella stood beside him, her heart beating in time with the growing pulse of the power around them. They had fought for so long, but the real battle was just beginning. The Night King's throne—the source of all the darkness—was still waiting, and with it, the final choice.

They had one chance to destroy it.

Together, they walked toward the spire, their steps heavy but purposeful, the weight of their past and the unknown future pressing down on them. The closer they came, the darker the air became, and the more the shadows seemed to close in on them, as if they were alive—watching, waiting for the moment when they would fail.

At the foot of the throne, the ground trembled beneath them. A low growl echoed through the air, a sound like distant thunder, as the shadows coalesced around them, thick and suffocating. The Night King's presence was still there, a lingering malevolence in the very stone, the earth, the air.

"Do you still feel it?" Mirella asked, her voice quiet, filled with the weight of all they had lost.

Riven nodded. "It's here. Waiting."

With a final, deep breath, Mirella turned to face him, her eyes meeting his with an intensity that burned brighter than any flame. "We've come this far," she whispered. "And we won't stop. We can't."

Riven's hand found hers, their fingers interlocking with the strength of a bond they had nearly lost. "No. We won't."

And together, they stepped forward into the heart of the darkness, determined to face whatever it took to break the curse once and for all.

Their love, their magic, and their will were the only things that could stop the Night King's reign of terror.

And as they reached the throne, the power they had unleashed together surged—silver and shadow, light and dark—clashing in a final, deafening explosion of energy.

Thirteen

The Moon's Embrace

The sky above had finally cleared, and the once-forsaken world was bathed in an ethereal glow. The moon, brighter than it had ever been, hung high above them, its silver light cascading over the broken landscape. Every shadow, every scar left in the wake of the battle seemed to be drawn to that light, as if the world itself were reaching toward it, seeking its warmth, its solace.

Mirella stood at the edge of the ruined throne, her body trembling, not from the cold, but from the weight of what had just transpired. The Night King was no more. His presence, that oppressive, suffocating force that had consumed them both, was gone. But the cost of that victory… the price they had paid… was now settling deep into their bones, into their hearts.

Beside her, Riven was silent. His shoulders were slumped, his hands still clenched at his sides, as if the echoes of the fight had left their marks on him that were deeper than any wound. His eyes were distant, lost in something Mirella couldn't quite reach. She could feel the pull of the bond between them, that connection they had fought so hard to protect, but there was something *different* now. Something raw, something jagged.

She reached out, her fingers brushing against his. His skin was warm, but the contact between them sent a shiver up her spine, the energy between them vibrating with an intensity that felt unfamiliar. A part of her wanted to pull back, to give him space, but another part of her, the part that had always been tethered to him, wanted to hold on.

"I didn't think…" Riven's voice was rough, like gravel scraping against stone. He turned to face her, his eyes darkened by the shadows of the past and the weight of the decisions they had made. "I didn't think it would end like this."

Mirella didn't know how to respond. What *could* she say? They had fought side by side, had sacrificed everything to break the curse, to stop the Night King, and yet, here they stood—alive, but irrevocably changed. Their bond had been tested to its breaking point, and though it had held, it had been forever altered.

"Neither did I," she whispered, her voice trembling as the weight of everything they had been through settled over her like a heavy fog. She wanted to say something more, to offer him comfort, but the truth was, she didn't know how to comfort *herself*, let alone him. They were both standing on the edge of something new, something unknown. The future stretched out before them like a vast, empty horizon.

"Do you feel it?" she asked softly, turning to face the horizon where the land stretched out before them, darkened by the aftershocks of the battle but lit by the moon's embrace. "The moon, Riven. It's *different*."

He glanced up at the sky, his gaze narrowing slightly as if trying to see what she saw. "The light… it's brighter than it ever was," he murmured. "But it feels distant."

Mirella nodded, her heart tightening. It was as though the world had been reshaped, the magic that had once thrummed through the land now lying dormant, like a vast ocean waiting for a spark. They had broken the curse, destroyed the Night King, but in the process, they had reshaped the very forces that governed their world. The moon's power, once a steady force that connected them, now seemed distant, unyielding.

"I don't know if we can ever truly heal from this," Riven said, his voice barely a whisper.

Mirella turned to him, her heart aching at the rawness of his words. She had been too afraid to admit it, but now, hearing him speak it aloud, it was as though the weight of it was too much to bear alone. The Night King's death had come at the expense of so much more than just their battle. It had changed the very fabric of the world. The magic was unstable now, the balance upended.

"It feels like… like we're in between worlds," Mirella said, her voice distant. "Like we're here, but not fully *here*. I don't know how to explain it, but it's like the world is still shifting beneath us."

Riven's expression softened as he stepped closer to her, his hand finding hers. "We've never been 'here,' Mirella. Not fully. Not in the way we should have been."

His words cut through her like a blade. He was right. She had never been able to shake the feeling that she was only a *part* of the world, that the world itself was always slipping through her fingers. She had fought for so long against the darkness, against the curse that bound them together, that she had never truly allowed herself to *be* with him, to be *here*, in the moment.

"I don't know how to fix this," she said, her voice trembling, her hand gripping his tighter. "I don't know how to fix what's been broken."

Riven's thumb brushed over her knuckles, his touch warm and comforting despite the distance between them. "Maybe we don't need to fix it. Maybe we just need to live with it."

She looked up at him, her heart swelling with a mixture of hope and fear. *Live with it.* Could they? Could they truly heal from the things they had endured? Could love, no matter how strong, save them from the weight of destiny? The world around them was healing, but it felt fragile. The bond they shared, though strong, felt like it had been shattered and put back together again—fragile, delicate.

"We've always been different, Mirella," Riven said, his voice low. "We've always walked a path that no one else could understand. But maybe... maybe that's what makes us strong. The fact that we've survived this far, despite everything."

Mirella's heart clenched at the thought. *Survived.* That was what they had done. They had *survived*—but at what cost?

"I don't know if I can keep going," she confessed, her voice barely a whisper. "I don't know if I can keep carrying this weight, the weight of everything we've lost."

Riven's expression softened, and he stepped closer, his hands gently cupping her face. "You don't have to carry it alone."

"I *want* to," she said, her voice breaking. "But I don't know how. I don't know how to go back to what we had. I don't know how to rebuild what was broken."

For a long moment, they simply stood there, their foreheads pressed together, the silence between them filled with the unspeakable weight of everything they had experienced. The magic of the moon shimmered above them, its light still dim but persistent. The land around them was still scarred, but it was healing. Slowly.

"You're right," Riven finally said, his voice steady, though laced with sadness. "We can't go back. We're not the same people we were before. The world isn't the same. But we're *here*, Mirella. And together, we'll face whatever comes next."

Mirella felt the truth of his words settle in her chest, a comfort despite the lingering ache of loss. She looked up at him, her gaze locking with his, and for the first time in what felt like an eternity, she allowed herself to simply *feel*—the love between them, the pain, the uncertainty. It was all there, wrapped in the quiet silence of the moment.

"We'll face it together," she whispered.

Riven smiled softly, though his eyes were still shadowed by the weight of everything they had experienced. "Always."

The world around them seemed to breathe in that moment. The land was quiet, the shadows retreating, the light of the moon brighter than ever before. It was as if the very earth itself had sighed in relief. And yet, despite the victory, despite the break in the curse, they both knew the truth.

The world was healing. But so were they. And it would take time. There were no simple answers. There would be no easy path forward. But as long as they had each other, as long as they walked through the storm together, they would find their way.

Riven stepped back slightly, his eyes never leaving hers. His hand slipped into hers, and the simple gesture was more than just comfort—it was a promise. A vow. To stand by each other, no matter what the future held.

Mirella closed her eyes for a moment, letting the peace of the moment wash over her. When she opened them again, the world around her seemed to shift, the light of the moon filling the world with a promise of something new. Something *better*. The weight of destiny, the curse, the battle—they had all been shattered.

Now, there was only the future.

And in that future, she and Riven would write their story. Not as victims of fate, but as the creators of their own destiny.

Together.

As the night stretched on, the moon's silver light bathed them in its gentle embrace, and the world seemed to breathe again.

And so did their love.

Fourteen

The Healer's Touch

The sun rose over the shattered landscape, painting the sky with hues of gold and crimson. It was the first dawn after the curse had been broken, the first light that seemed to cleanse the world of the darkness that had plagued it for centuries. The land, still scarred by the battles fought in its name, slowly began to show signs of life again—small patches of greenery sprouting through the cracked earth, streams of clear water rushing where there had once been only desolate wasteland.

Mirella stood at the edge of a clearing, her heart full as she watched the horizon. The warmth of the sun on her skin felt different now—gentler, softer—almost as if the world itself were offering them a second chance. But there was a weight to the new day, a reminder of everything they had lost and the cost of their victory. The air hummed with potential, but it also thrummed with the remnants of the past, echoes of the curse that still clung to them, even in the moments when the world seemed to be healing.

Her fingers lightly brushed the glowing sigil on her chest, the symbol that had once bound her and Riven together. The sigil had faded after the curse had been broken, its once-vibrant glow now a faint echo, like the memory of a dream. It no longer burned with the same intensity, but Mirella knew it was still there, still a part of her—part of her journey, part of the bond they had shared. A bond that had shaped them, broken them, and ultimately healed them.

She glanced at Riven, who stood nearby, his back to her as he gazed out at the land. The shadows that had once clung to him so tightly were no longer there. The oppressive darkness that had defined him, controlled him, was gone, replaced by a quiet peace that seemed to radiate from him. He had shed the weight of his heritage, the curse that had haunted him his entire life. And though the scars of his past remained, there was a lightness in his step now, a sense of freedom that had been absent before.

Mirella's heart swelled with a deep, unspoken affection as she watched him, but there was something more—something darker that lingered in the depths of her own soul. She had broken the curse, but in doing so, she had uncovered something about herself that terrified her. The magic that had always been inside her, the light that had connected her to the moon, had grown stronger since the battle. And with that power came a responsibility she wasn't sure she was ready for.

Her breath caught in her throat as she took a tentative step forward, her feet sinking into the soft earth beneath her. The power was still there, thrumming beneath her skin, a fire that could burn just as easily as it could heal. The day she had spent learning to control it had been filled with triumphs, but also doubts. She had healed small wounds, mended broken branches, coaxed life back into the soil, but the real challenge was yet to come. The magic was so strong now, it frightened her. It was wild and untamed, much like the darkness she had once fought.

She had been born with the ability to heal, to mend what was broken, but now, it felt like she was standing on the edge of something much bigger. Every time she called upon the magic, she felt the weight of it pressing against her, threatening to swallow her whole. What if she couldn't control it? What if she lost herself in the power, just as Riven had lost himself in the shadows?

Her thoughts were interrupted by Riven's voice, soft but steady, cutting through the silence.

"Mirella."

She turned toward him, her heart skipping a beat at the look in his eyes. There was something in his gaze—a depth of understanding, of shared pain—that made her feel as though he could see through her, into the very heart of her fears.

"You're thinking too much," Riven said gently, his voice a quiet rumble in the stillness of the morning.

Mirella hesitated. She didn't want to burden him with her doubts. Not after everything they had been through. But there was no hiding it—not from him.

"I'm scared," she admitted, her voice barely above a whisper. "I don't know if I can control this magic. I don't know what it could do if I lose myself to it."

Riven stepped closer, his eyes never leaving hers. "You've always had it within you. The magic—it's a part of you. Just as much as the light inside you is a part of me."

Mirella swallowed hard, her chest tightening. "But what if it's too much? What if I *break*?"

Riven reached out, his hand brushing against hers, his touch a steady anchor. "You won't. Not while I'm here."

She met his gaze, searching for the truth in his words. There was no doubt in his eyes, no hint of hesitation. He had fought his own demons, battled his own darkness, and now, he was offering her the same trust. The same strength.

"I'm scared of losing control," she said, the words spilling out before she could stop them. "What if I become like the Night King? What if I let the magic consume me?"

Riven's expression softened. "You won't. You're not him, Mirella. You're not bound by fate like he was. You've always been free. You're choosing to use your power for good, and that's what makes you different."

Mirella closed her eyes, letting the quiet of the world wash over her, letting the soothing energy of Riven's words settle in her heart. He was right. She had *always* chosen. And that was what had made her different, what had kept her from losing herself in the darkness. She wasn't defined by the magic within her. She was defined by the choices she made. By the love she gave. By the life she chose to build.

Taking a deep breath, she opened her eyes. "I want to heal, Riven. I want to help. But I don't want to lose myself in the process."

He smiled then, a soft, knowing smile. "You won't. You have me, Mirella. Always."

For a long moment, they stood there, the sun climbing higher in the sky, the warmth of the light filling the world around them. Mirella felt the weight of the past lifting, but it was replaced by something else—something even heavier.

Responsibility. A duty to protect what they had rebuilt, to nurture the world that had been broken, just as she had once been.

"I want to try," she said, her voice filled with resolve. "I want to learn how to use this power to heal—not just the land, but people. I want to give them hope again."

Riven's gaze softened, and he nodded. "You already have, Mirella. You've given me hope. You've given all of us hope."

She smiled at him, the weight of his words filling her with a quiet strength. They had fought side by side, had sacrificed everything to get here. And now, together, they would build something new. They would heal the land. They would heal each other.

Mirella's hand lifted, her fingers brushing the air as she called upon the magic within her, feeling the connection to the earth, to the world, to the moon. The magic surged through her, warm and steady, like a pulse beneath her skin. She could feel the energy flowing through her, the power of the earth and the moon, intertwining with her own.

The magic was still wild, still untamed, but now, she felt its warmth instead of its weight. She could feel the land beneath her, the heartbeat of the world. With each breath, she could hear the whisper of the trees, the song of the rivers, the call of the creatures that had returned with the healing of the earth. The power was there, but it was no longer something to fear. It was a part of her. And it was *her choice* how to use it.

A small branch near her foot shifted, the leaves trembling as if alive. She smiled, her fingers glowing with soft silver light as she gently coaxed the energy from within her into the earth. The branch straightened, the leaves shimmering with newfound vitality. Slowly, a new flower bloomed at its tip, delicate and pure, the first of many.

"Mirella," Riven said softly, his voice filled with wonder.

She turned to him, her smile brightening. "It's working."

He stepped closer, his hand reaching out to gently take hers. "You're incredible."

She laughed softly, her heart light. "We are, Riven. Together."

As they stood there, watching the world begin to heal, Mirella realized something—*they* had changed. The world had changed. The magic inside her had changed. But there was one thing that had remained constant through it all.

Their love.

The bond that had been tested by fire, by darkness, by pain, was stronger than ever. And now, as they stood in the warmth of the sun, bathed in the light of the moon, she knew that no matter what lay ahead, they would face it together.

For the first time in so long, Mirella allowed herself to truly *believe* in their future.

Together, they would write a new story.

And it would be one of healing, of hope, and of love.

The afternoon sun hung lazily in the sky, casting golden hues across the rolling fields that stretched beyond the ruins of what had once been the Night King's domain. The land was scarred but not lifeless. Wildflowers began to peek through the fractured earth, small tendrils of ivy creeping up the broken stones of once-shadowed structures. The air no longer carried the weight of despair, though whispers of magic still lingered, weaving between the trees, waiting.

Mirella knelt beside a wounded traveler at the edge of the village, her hands hovering just above the deep wound in his side. The man, a soldier from a distant kingdom, had been found collapsed near the river, his armor cracked, his face etched with exhaustion. Riven stood beside her, silent, watchful. He no longer carried the tension he once had—the fear of losing himself to the darkness—but there was still something cautious in his stance, as if he were waiting for the moment her magic would overwhelm her.

She exhaled slowly, steadying herself. She had been practicing, learning to temper the raw power that coursed through her veins. The moon's magic had grown within her, and now it called to her, whispering that she could *do more, be more,* but she had to keep control. This was different from battle. This was not a fight for survival but a test of trust—of faith in herself.

She placed her palms over the wound, ignoring the stickiness of blood that stained his tunic. A soft glow emanated from her fingertips, silver tendrils of light weaving through the wound, knitting torn flesh together. The man gasped, his body shuddering as the magic worked through him, but Mirella held firm, pushing just enough energy to mend him without losing herself in it.

When the light dimmed, only a faint scar remained where there had once been an open wound.

The soldier blinked, dazed. "I—" His voice cracked as he tried to speak, but his throat was dry.

"Easy," Mirella murmured, offering him a water flask. "You're safe now."

He took it hesitantly, his gaze shifting between her and Riven, uncertainty flickering behind his eyes. "I've never seen healing like that before. Not even from the priestesses of Avelon."

Mirella smiled, though there was a hint of exhaustion in her eyes. "It's new to me too," she admitted.

The soldier drank deeply, then looked toward the horizon, his brow furrowing. "They said the Night King was gone, that the curse was broken, but… I can still feel something. A weight in the air."

Mirella stiffened. She had felt it too. It was subtle, like a faint echo, a presence that should not be there but still lingered on the edges of perception.

Riven spoke for the first time, his voice calm but firm. "The darkness doesn't vanish overnight. The world is still healing. It will take time."

The soldier nodded slowly. "Then let us hope the world has enough of it."

As he stood, testing his newly healed strength, Mirella felt Riven's hand rest lightly against her lower back. A silent reassurance. She leaned into his touch just slightly, taking comfort in the quiet solidarity between them.

When the soldier had gone, disappearing down the path that led toward the rebuilt village, Riven finally spoke again.

"You're getting stronger," he said, his voice low.

Mirella looked up at him, searching his face for any trace of fear or doubt. She found none. Only quiet admiration.

"It's not just me that's changing," she replied. "You're different too."

Riven exhaled, his fingers brushing absently against the hilt of his blade, though there was no threat near them now. It had once been a reflex—always ready for a fight, always expecting danger. But now, his stance was looser, his grip lighter. He was learning to live without the weight of the curse pressing down on him.

"I don't know who I am without the darkness," he admitted after a long silence. "I spent so long fighting it, fearing it, and now that it's gone… I don't know what's left."

Mirella turned to face him fully, reaching for his hand. "You're *you*, Riven. Not just the warrior, not just the cursed prince. Just *you*."

His expression softened, though his eyes still held the weight of uncertainty. "And what if that's not enough?"

Mirella squeezed his hand. "It's more than enough."

For the first time in what felt like years, Riven allowed himself to believe her.

They spent the next few days rebuilding. Not just the village, but themselves. Mirella worked tirelessly, using her powers to heal the wounded, to restore the land, but she was careful. She set limits for herself, knowing now that magic was a gift, but one that could consume if wielded without restraint.

Riven, too, found his place—not as a warrior bound to fight a never-ending battle, but as something *more*. He helped the villagers, trained those who wished to protect themselves, and learned how to exist without constantly being at war with himself. The nightmares still came sometimes—shadows clawing at the edges of his mind—but each time he awoke, Mirella was there. And that was enough.

One evening, beneath the light of the full moon, they stood at the river's edge. The water was calm, reflecting the silver light above, the night air carrying the soft scent of blooming jasmine.

Mirella tilted her head back, letting the moon's glow wash over her, feeling the steady hum of power within her. It no longer burned with a wild intensity. It was quieter now, settled within her like a heartbeat.

Riven watched her, his gaze unreadable. "Do you still feel it?" he asked.

She nodded. "It's different now. It doesn't control me. It's just… part of me."

He reached out, brushing a strand of hair from her face. "And do you regret it? Any of it?"

Mirella turned to him, meeting his gaze, searching for the answer she already knew in her heart. There was pain in their past, scars that would never fully fade, but there was also love—something stronger than magic, stronger than fate.

"No," she said softly. "I don't regret any of it. Because it brought me to you."

Riven exhaled, a slow, almost disbelieving sound, before he pulled her into his arms. His embrace was warm, solid, grounding her in a way that nothing else could. She felt his heartbeat against hers, steady and real.

"You once asked me what comes after the curse," he murmured against her hair.

She remembered that night. The fear in his voice. The uncertainty. And now, standing here, in the light of the moon, she finally had an answer.

"We live," she whispered. "We heal. And we *choose* what comes next."

Riven pulled back slightly, just enough to look into her eyes. And for the first time, she saw something there that hadn't been there before.

Hope.

A slow, small smile tugged at his lips. "Then let's choose *together*."

Mirella smiled back, leaning into him as the river whispered its song and the stars above bore witness to the love that had endured the darkest of nights.

And in the quiet, in the peace they had fought so hard to

earn, she knew that whatever came next—whether light or darkness—they would face it side by side.

Together. Always.

Fifteen

The Shifting Stars

The wind was heavy with the scent of fresh earth, carrying with it the promise of rebirth. The land, still scarred from the battle with the Night King, was slowly beginning to heal. Fields that had once been barren now sprouted with new life—wildflowers bloomed in vibrant clusters, and the river's waters ran clearer than they had in centuries. Even the trees, stripped bare of their leaves by the shadow's touch, were beginning to sprout fresh shoots, reaching toward the sun in quiet defiance of the darkness that had once ruled them.

But for all the beauty that surrounded them, there was an undercurrent of tension, a growing sense that the peace they had fought so hard to achieve was fragile. The world was healing, yes, but deep within the earth, beneath the roots and rivers, something still stirred. An ancient presence, older than the curse they had broken, seemed to be waking.

Mirella stood at the edge of the forest, her hand pressed against the rough bark of an oak tree, her senses reaching out, as if trying to connect with the land. She could feel the magic in the air, the pulse of life returning, but beneath it, there was something else. A tremor, like a heartbeat in the earth, something dark and patient. It was as though the world was holding its breath, waiting.

"Are you feeling it too?" Riven's voice came from behind her, low and steady, a thread of concern weaving through his words.

Mirella didn't turn to face him. Instead, she nodded. "Something's wrong. The land is healing, but it's not… whole. There's a rippling in the magic, a disturbance I can't explain."

Riven moved closer, standing beside her. His presence was comforting, but she could feel the weight of the unspoken worry between them. He was still struggling, trying to find his place in this new world that no longer depended on his shadowed past. But Mirella had always believed in the strength of their bond—*their* ability to overcome whatever the world threw at them, together.

"We've been through worse," Riven said, his voice tinged with both resolve and exhaustion. "But this feels different. Whatever it is, it's not from the Night King. It's something older, deeper."

Mirella closed her eyes for a moment, letting the wind brush against her skin, feeling the pull of the world around her. The earth hummed beneath her fingertips, a vibration that ran through her very bones. It was a reminder that everything was connected—that the power they wielded, the magic they had fought for, was part of something much larger than themselves.

"We need to find out what this is," she said finally, her voice a quiet determination. "Before it finds us."

A low growl rumbled in the distance, cutting through the tension in the air. Mirella stiffened, her heart skipping a beat as her senses flared to life. Riven's hand instinctively moved to the hilt of his blade, and she knew he was ready to defend her—just as he always had. But this time, something felt different.

"We're not alone," she whispered, her eyes narrowing as she scanned the forest around them.

The sound grew louder, and as it did, figures began to emerge from the trees—strange shapes, shadows that twisted and flickered in the shifting moonlight. Mirella's breath caught as she recognized the figures stepping into the clearing.

It wasn't just the two of them facing whatever threat lay ahead. It was an army.

Riven stiffened beside her. "Who are they?"

Mirella took a step forward, her heart racing, but her voice calm. "I don't know. But I have a feeling we're about to find out."

The first of the figures stepped fully into view—a tall, lithe woman, her skin shimmering with an ethereal glow. She wore armor made from leaves and vines, a crown of silver leaves resting lightly upon her head. Her eyes gleamed like pools of liquid gold, the light of the moon reflecting in them.

She was beautiful, ancient, and unearthly.

"Do not be alarmed," the woman's voice rang out, clear and resonant, like the sound of a bell tolling in the distance. "We are the Keepers of the Veil."

Mirella's heart stilled. The name sent a shiver down her spine.

"The Keepers of the Veil," Riven repeated, his brow furrowing. "I've heard legends of you. The guardians of the boundaries between worlds."

The woman nodded, her golden eyes never leaving them. "Yes. The Veil between the worlds of light and shadow has thinned. And it is because of your actions, Mirella, and Riven, that the balance has been disturbed. You have broken the Night King's hold on the earth, but something darker has awakened in the shadows."

Mirella's mind raced. "What do you mean? We defeated the Night King. The curse is broken. The darkness is gone."

"Not all of it," the woman said softly. "What you faced was only one part of an ancient force, a remnant of an even greater power. And now, that power seeks to undo all that you have worked for."

Riven's hand tightened on the hilt of his sword, his body tense. "What is it that we're up against?"

The woman stepped forward, her gaze never wavering. "The Starborn."

Mirella blinked, confusion furrowing her brow. "The Starborn?"

"Yes," the woman replied, her voice laced with sorrow. "An ancient force that predates even the Night King's bloodline. They were born from the darkness between the stars, from the places where the realms converge. The Starborn are the true origin of the curse you broke."

Riven exchanged a glance with Mirella, his expression hardening. "You're saying the curse wasn't just a product of the Night King? That something older is at play?"

The woman nodded gravely. "The curse you defeated was only one piece of the puzzle. The Starborn are ancient, and they are awakening once more. They seek to return to the world of light and reclaim what was once theirs."

Mirella felt a chill race through her, the weight of the woman's words settling in her chest. "And what does that mean for us?"

"You cannot defeat them with force alone," the woman warned. "The Starborn are beyond the reach of normal magic. Their power is drawn from the very fabric of reality itself. They are the shadows between the stars—the force that holds all worlds in balance."

Riven stepped forward, his eyes dark with determination. "Then what can we do? How do we stop them?"

The woman's gaze softened for the briefest of moments. "You must seek the Heart of the Veil—the place where the worlds meet. Only there can you confront the Starborn and restore the balance. But be warned: the path is fraught with danger. The Veil has been weakened, and what lies on the other side is a place of nightmares."

Mirella's pulse quickened. "And how do we find it?"

"You will not be alone," the woman said, raising her hand. "We will guide you, for the Keepers of the Veil are sworn to protect the balance. But you must act quickly, for the Starborn are already moving, already preparing to return."

A rustle sounded in the trees, and a group of warriors, equally as ethereal and striking as the woman, stepped forward. Their armor glinted with the light of stars, and their eyes glowed with a faint, otherworldly fire. Mirella's breath caught in her throat. These were no ordinary warriors. They were beings of the Veil, of the very magic that held the worlds together.

"You will need our strength," the woman continued. "And you will need more than just your own power. The Veil is not just a place—it is a *force*, and you must harness its energy to stand a chance."

Mirella looked up at Riven, her heart pounding in her chest. A new battle was ahead of them, one that would take them beyond the world they knew, beyond even the power they had already wielded. The shadows were shifting once again, this time with a darkness more ancient and primal than anything they had faced before.

But they were not alone. They had allies, warriors who understood the ancient forces at play.

"We'll do whatever it takes," Mirella said, her voice steady with a determination she hadn't felt in a long time.

The woman nodded, and for the first time, there was something like a smile on her lips. "Then let us begin."

And with that, Mirella, Riven, and their newfound allies turned toward the unknown, toward the heart of the Veil where the stars themselves trembled, waiting to be awakened.

And in the distance, the stars shifted, their paths altering as the ancient forces began to stir once again. The true battle had only just begun.

The moon, once a constant companion in the sky, now hung like a silent witness, its light flickering faintly in the growing darkness. The world around them seemed to hum with quiet tension, a collective breath being held as if the land itself were waiting for the coming storm. The stars overhead, once brilliant and untouchable, now seemed strangely close, as if they had shifted, slipping into alignment with the growing force that had begun to stir.

Mirella's heart raced as she and Riven followed the Keepers of the Veil through the dense forest, their footsteps muffled by the soft carpet of moss beneath them. Each step carried them deeper into the unknown, into a realm where the rules of magic were twisted, where the threads of fate hung loosely and were more easily severed than they ever could have imagined.

The path ahead was dark, the trees towering above them like ancient sentinels. The air smelled of damp earth, of life and decay woven together. The warriors of the Veil moved with an otherworldly grace, their movements fluid and silent, as though they were more part of the forest than individuals themselves.

Riven's hand brushed against Mirella's, the touch a subtle reminder of the bond they shared, fragile yet unbreakable. He hadn't spoken much since their conversation with the Keepers, but she could feel the unspoken weight of the journey ahead pressing on him. His past—the darkness that had always threatened to swallow him—was still a part of him. She could feel it lingering beneath the surface, just as she could still sense the pull of her own powers, as wild and untamed as the land around them.

"Mirella," Riven's voice came, low and quiet, a thread of concern woven through the calmness. "I can't shake the feeling that we're being watched."

She nodded, her eyes scanning the shadows ahead of them, the uneasy sensation growing in her chest. It wasn't the first time they'd felt it—the sense that something was following them, watching, waiting. The night had become alive with unseen presences, each flicker of movement behind them a reminder that they weren't alone in this. The world was healing, yes, but some parts of it were still broken, and the darkness had not relinquished its hold entirely.

"We are," Mirella replied, her voice tinged with unease. "But the Veil itself is an unstable place. The magic that holds it together is weakening. It attracts things—things that shouldn't be here."

Riven's grip on her hand tightened. "And we're walking straight into the heart of it."

The tension between them was palpable, like a thin thread stretched taut, ready to snap at any moment. Mirella's heart pounded in her chest as they moved forward, the path ahead becoming darker, the shadows more oppressive. She could feel the weight of the magic in the air, the pull of the Veil growing stronger with every step.

After what felt like hours, they reached a clearing, the moon now a pale sliver in the sky. The stars above them shone brighter here, as if drawing them into their light, their energy. At the center of the clearing stood a structure unlike anything Mirella had ever seen. It was a temple of sorts, but not built by human hands. The walls shimmered with a silver-blue light, etched with symbols that seemed to writhe and shift as if alive. The stones beneath their feet hummed with an ancient power, a force that seemed to stretch across time itself.

The Keepers stepped forward, their faces solemn, their movements precise. The woman with the crown of silver leaves raised her hand, and the symbols on the temple walls flared with light, the magic bending to her will. The air grew thick, charged with an energy that made Mirella's skin prickle.

"This is the Heart of the Veil," the woman said, her voice reverberating through the clearing. "Where the worlds meet and part. It is here that the Starborn seek to break through."

Mirella felt a shiver run down her spine as the weight of her words sank in. The Heart of the Veil. It was a place of power, of magic older than time itself. And yet, despite its beauty, despite the serenity it projected, there was a palpable sense of foreboding here, as if something dark was watching from just beyond the edges of perception.

"Are we ready?" Riven asked quietly, his gaze fixed on the temple before them.

Mirella nodded, her grip tightening on his hand. "We have no choice."

The Keepers began their chant, their voices rising in a low, rhythmic hum. The symbols on the temple walls pulsed in time with their words, and the air around them grew thick with magic. Mirella closed her eyes, feeling the energy swell around her, an almost tangible force that pulled at her insides.

And then, as if in response to their chant, the earth beneath them trembled. The wind howled through the trees, the leaves swirling in a frenzy. Mirella's heart skipped a beat, and her senses flared with sudden, overwhelming urgency.

"Something's coming," she said, her voice tight with fear.

The stars above them flickered, as if shaken by an unseen hand, their paths shifting in unnatural ways. The once-still air crackled with power, and the ground beneath them seemed to pulse with a rhythm that wasn't their own. Riven stepped closer to her, his sword drawn, his body poised for action.

The Keepers chanted louder, their voices becoming more urgent. The symbols on the temple walls began to shift rapidly, flashing in an array of patterns, each one more complex than the last.

Suddenly, the air exploded with light.

A figure emerged from the shimmering vortex, a tall, shadowed silhouette that seemed to materialize from the very darkness of the Veil itself. The stars above them screamed in a haunting chorus, their light faltering as the figure stepped fully into the clearing. It was humanoid, its form tall and impossibly thin, its skin like obsidian, reflecting no light. Eyes like molten silver burned from beneath a crown of twisted, star-like shards.

Mirella's breath caught in her throat. This was it. This was the true force they had been warned about—the Starborn. The creatures born of the night between the stars, whose power could unravel the very fabric of reality itself.

The figure raised its hand, and the magic in the air rippled, distorting the space around them. The trees seemed to bend and twist, the ground shifting beneath their feet. The air grew thick with the weight of it, the overwhelming pressure of something ancient, something primordial.

"You have come far, mortal ones," the Starborn intoned, its voice a soft whisper that seemed to echo from everywhere and nowhere all at once. "But you cannot stop what is inevitable."

Mirella felt the darkness pressing against her, the force of it suffocating her, trying to pull her down, back into the abyss from which it had emerged. She struggled to keep her focus, to keep her strength, but it was so overwhelming, so vast. She could feel Riven beside her, his presence grounding her, but she knew that they could not face this alone. The force of the Starborn was too great.

"Stop!" she shouted, her voice trembling, but her determination unyielding. "We won't let you undo what we've fought for!"

The Starborn's laugh was low, chilling, the sound reverberating through the night like the echo of thunder.

"You think you can fight fate?" it said, its voice like the hiss of a serpent. "You are but children playing with forces far beyond your understanding."

But even as it spoke, Mirella felt the power of the moon rise within her, the magic that had always been a part of her, now swirling with more intensity than ever before. She couldn't lose herself to this darkness. Not after everything they had sacrificed.

And beside her, she could feel Riven's strength, his heart beating with hers in a steady rhythm, steady and strong.

"We're not children," Riven said, his voice sharp and unwavering. "We've faced darkness before. And we *will* face you."

Mirella turned to him, and for the first time since they had begun this journey, she felt a true surge of power. Together, they had faced impossible odds. Together, they had won. And together, they would win again.

The magic between them flared, silver light crackling through the air as they focused their combined strength, pouring everything they had into a single, desperate attack.

The Starborn recoiled, its eyes narrowing as the magic struck. But it was only the beginning. The night had just begun to shift, and with it, the battle for the future had truly begun.

And the stakes were higher than they could have ever imagined.

Sixteen

The Circle Reborn

T he wind howled through the jagged peaks of the mountain range, its cry a haunting reminder of the journey still ahead. The air was thin, carrying the chill of the ancient world—of a time before time, when the earth itself had been shaped by the will of the gods. Mirella pulled her cloak tighter around her shoulders, the fabric rippling in the harsh gusts. Beside her, Riven moved with quiet determination, his silhouette cutting through the mist like a shadow made flesh. The path ahead was treacherous, winding through the rocky terrain, leading them to the heart of the world—the place where everything had begun.

The pieces of the ancient artifact they needed to restore peace were scattered across the world, hidden in places of untold power. Each piece was a key, a crucial fragment that would unlock the final seal on the darkness that had threatened to consume the world for so long. But the journey to retrieve them had not been easy. Along the way, they had faced dangers that tested not only their strength but their very resolve.

And now, they stood on the precipice of the final test.

Mirella could feel the weight of the world pressing down on her, the magic that had flowed through her veins since the moment she had broken the curse pulsing beneath her skin. She had learned to wield it, to control it, but it was a constant battle. Each time she used the power, it felt as if she were walking a tightrope, balancing between light and dark, love and loss. It had been the most difficult lesson of her life, but it had also been the most freeing. She had learned that the true power was not in the magic itself, but in the choices they made. And every choice she had made, she had made with Riven.

Beside her, Riven seemed to carry a similar weight, though his struggles were different. The darkness that had once ruled him, the curse that had bound him to a fate of despair, was gone. Yet, there were scars—deep, hidden scars—that would never fade. Mirella knew that Riven's greatest battle was not against the darkness outside, but against the darkness within himself. He had fought to be free, to prove he was not bound by the bloodline that had cursed him. But sometimes, in the quiet moments between their battles, she could see the shadow of doubt that flickered behind his eyes.

"Are you ready?" she asked softly, her voice barely above the roar of the wind.

Riven didn't look at her immediately, his gaze fixed on the path ahead. The peaks of the mountain loomed above them like silent giants, their jagged edges cutting into the sky. The air was growing colder, the farther they traveled. A storm was brewing, an omen of the trials to come.

"As ready as I'll ever be," he replied, his voice low, but steady.

"I won't let anything take you from me. Not now. Not ever."

Mirella smiled, though the tension in her chest remained. She reached for his hand, her fingers curling around his with the familiar comfort that only Riven could provide. They had faced so much, and yet, there was a finality to this journey that made everything feel different—like the end of something, and the beginning of something else.

The path twisted, narrowing as they approached the heart of the mountain. The wind carried the scent of ancient earth, the smell of something both old and alive, a reminder that the world was not just a place of stone and dust—it was alive, pulsing with the same magic that ran through them. Mirella could feel the pull of it, like a heartbeat in the distance, drawing her forward, urging her onward.

They reached a massive stone archway carved into the side of the mountain—a door that seemed to pulse with ancient power. Symbols, etched in forgotten languages, spiraled around the edges, glowing faintly in the dim light. The air around them hummed with a strange energy, and the ground beneath their feet seemed to tremble with the weight of untold magic.

"This is it," Riven said, his voice a mixture of awe and apprehension. "The heart of the world."

Mirella stepped forward, her heart pounding in her chest. She could feel the weight of the artifact pieces, each one a fragment of the power that had once ruled the world. The final piece was here, hidden within the very heart of the mountain, protected by forces that no mortal had ever dared challenge. She could feel the magic around them, ancient and untamed, pressing in on all sides.

Riven stepped beside her, his presence steadying her, as they moved toward the archway. The symbols on the stone glowed brighter as they approached, and the air grew heavier with each step. They had come this far. They had fought against the shadows, against the darkness that sought to consume everything they loved. But now, standing on the threshold of the final battle, Mirella couldn't shake the feeling that something more was at play here—something neither she nor Riven could have anticipated.

A voice, deep and resonant, echoed from within the stone arch. "You seek the final piece, the key to restoring balance. But what you have yet to understand is that the balance comes at a price. A price that cannot be paid by magic alone."

Mirella froze, her eyes scanning the darkness within the archway. The voice seemed to come from everywhere, wrapping around them like tendrils of mist.

"Who are you?" she called out, her voice steady despite the growing unease that tightened in her chest.

"We are the keepers of the Circle," the voice replied. "We are the ones who maintain the balance. The key you seek is not just a tool to restore what was broken. It is the key to a cycle. A cycle that must be completed before the world can heal."

The ground beneath them trembled again, and the symbols on the archway flared with bright light, casting long shadows across the ground. Mirella could feel the pull of the magic, like a tide that was about to crash over them, overwhelming them.

"Complete the cycle?" Riven asked, his voice taut with suspicion. "What do you mean?"

"The darkness you fought," the voice said, growing softer now, as if it were drawing closer. "It was not an accident. It was not a singular event. It is part of a pattern. A pattern of death and rebirth, of light and shadow. You, Mirella, you and Riven, are not just the healers of the world. You are the ones who will decide whether the cycle ends or continues. The artifact you seek will restore balance, yes, but only if you choose to complete the circle."

Mirella's heart raced, confusion flooding her thoughts. She turned to Riven, searching his face for answers. But his expression mirrored her own—uncertainty, fear, and a deep, nagging sense that they were standing on the edge of something they couldn't fully understand.

"What price?" she asked, her voice barely above a whisper.

"The price," the voice said, a ripple of finality in its tone, "is the one you have carried all along. The burden of your love. For love is what binds the circle. Without it, balance cannot be restored."

Mirella's breath caught. "Our love?" she asked, disbelief creeping into her voice. "You want us to sacrifice—"

"Not sacrifice," the voice interrupted, gentle now. "But to accept the true nature of your bond. It is not just a gift, nor a weapon. It is the essence of the circle—the force that will either end the cycle of darkness or perpetuate it."

Riven stepped forward, his jaw set with resolve. "What do we need to do?"

"You must place the last piece of the artifact within the circle," the voice said, its tone now thick with power. "But when you do, the choice will be made. The circle will close, and the world will either heal or fall."

Mirella's heart pounded in her chest as she glanced at Riven. They had already sacrificed so much. Could they truly accept what they were being asked to do?

"Together," she whispered, taking his hand, her voice steady. "Whatever happens, we do this together."

Riven squeezed her hand, a fire in his eyes that matched her own. "Always."

And with that, they stepped forward, their hearts united as they moved toward the center of the archway, where the final piece of the artifact waited. The moment their fingers touched the stone, the world seemed to shift. Magic surged, flowing through them, and the world around them began to bend, as if the very fabric of reality were being rewoven by their touch.

The symbols on the stone glowed brighter, flooding the clearing with light as they placed the final piece into the center of the circle. The air cracked with energy, the winds whipping around them in a frenzy.

And in that moment, the choice was made.

The circle was reborn.

But as the light faded, Mirella and Riven felt a new force surging through them—a power, both ancient and new, that they couldn't yet comprehend. The darkness that had threatened the world had been halted, but a new cycle had begun. A cycle that was theirs to shape.

The heart of the world had been healed.

But the true test was only just beginning.

The world seemed to hold its breath.

Mirella felt it first, the subtle shift beneath her feet, the way the very earth seemed to vibrate with the energy of the circle they had completed. The light from the stone faded, leaving only the quiet glow of the moon overhead. For a moment, everything was still—eerily still. The wind no longer howled through the trees, and the air hung heavy with a sense of finality, as if time itself had paused to witness their decision.

She glanced at Riven, their fingers still intertwined. His eyes met hers, dark with understanding and concern, but there was something else in them too—a quiet acceptance, a shared strength that had always been there, even in the darkest of times. Their bond, forged in the fires of battle and tempered in the shadow of the curse, had become something deeper, something unbreakable. Whatever lay ahead, they would face it together.

"Did we do it?" she whispered, her voice tinged with uncertainty.

Riven nodded slowly, his gaze fixed on the stone in the center of the circle. "I think so. But we don't know yet. We don't know what the cost will be."

Mirella's heart skipped a beat as she looked down at the stone, now completely still. She could feel the hum of magic within her, pulsing with the energy of the artifact, but something was different. There was no immediate burst of light, no overwhelming rush of power. Instead, it was as if the magic had settled, like a deep breath taken after a long, agonizing battle.

And then, the earth began to stir again.

At first, it was a tremor, barely perceptible beneath her feet. But it quickly grew stronger, the ground shaking violently beneath them. Mirella stumbled, her hand reaching out to steady herself, but the force of the tremor was too much. Riven's arm shot out to catch her, his grip firm, but even he struggled to keep his footing.

"What's happening?" Mirella gasped, panic rising in her chest.

"I don't know!" Riven's voice was tight with alarm. "This wasn't part of the plan. The balance should have been restored!"

The sky above them darkened, as though a cloud had passed

over the moon. The stars flickered, their positions shifting unnaturally, as if something were distorting the very fabric of the heavens. Mirella's stomach churned with the realization—this was not the peace they had hoped for. This was the aftermath of a choice made, but the consequences were still unfolding.

From the darkness came a low, rumbling voice, deep and resonant, as if it came from the very core of the world itself.

"The Circle has been reborn," the voice intoned. "But the cost of restoring balance is not yet paid. You, who have chosen the path of the Light, must now face the true weight of your decision."

Mirella's breath hitched. Her eyes darted around the clearing, searching for the source of the voice, but there was nothing. No figure, no shadow. Just the shifting stars above and the trembling earth beneath.

"Who are you?" Riven demanded, his voice steady despite the tension in the air. "What do you want from us?"

"The cost of the Circle's rebirth is not in the artifact alone," the voice continued, its tone mocking and full of ancient power. "The true price is a life, a soul bound to the light and shadow. The Circle demands its sacrifice. And you, Mirella and Riven, are the ones who must pay it."

A cold wave of realization washed over Mirella. Her heart raced as she turned to Riven, searching his face for any sign of understanding.

"No," she whispered, her voice cracking. "No, we've already sacrificed so much. I—I can't lose you. Not now."

Riven's expression remained calm, though there was a flicker of something dark behind his eyes. He gripped her hands tighter, his voice low but steady. "Mirella, we don't know what this is. We don't know if this is the true cost. But we've already faced worse. Whatever this is, we'll face it together."

But even as he spoke, Mirella felt the world shifting again, the ground beneath them rumbling more violently now. The stars above them flared with unnatural light, casting long shadows across the land. Something was coming—a force greater than either of them had imagined.

Suddenly, the ground cracked open beneath their feet, the earth splitting wide, sending a shockwave of magic that threw them both to the ground. Mirella gasped as she tumbled, her body landing hard against the jagged rocks. Her vision blurred for a moment as the world spun around her, the echoes of the rumbling earth filling her ears.

When she opened her eyes again, she was alone.

Riven was gone.

Panic surged through her chest as she scrambled to her feet, her heart pounding. "Riven!" she called, her voice hoarse, desperate. But the words fell into the oppressive silence around her, swallowed by the growing darkness.

The earth was split wide, a chasm stretching out before her, glowing with a dark, sickly light. From within the depths of the chasm, a figure emerged—tall, shadowed, and impossibly ancient. Its eyes were black voids, the pupils nothing more than pinpricks of light, flickering like dying stars.

"You have chosen the Circle," the figure said, its voice a low rasp. "But the balance requires more than mere mortals. It requires a sacrifice that neither love nor magic can save you from. The Circle demands its price."

Mirella stumbled backward, her heart racing. "What is it? What do you want from us?"

The figure's hollow eyes fixed on her with an intensity that sent chills through her bones. "It is not what *I* want, child. It is what the Circle demands. The Light and the Shadow, bound by your bond, are the only ones who can restore balance. But balance is not a gift—it is a constant exchange. For every life, a life must be lost. For every light, a shadow must fall. The Circle is complete, but the price must still be paid."

Mirella's breath caught in her throat as the figure moved closer, its form flickering in and out of existence like a shadow cast by the faintest light. "No," she whispered, shaking her head, refusing to believe it. "You can't take him. We've given everything. We've *fought* for this."

"You have fought," the figure replied, its voice carrying an ancient sorrow. "But you are not the first to break the Circle. And you will not be the last."

Mirella's hands trembled as she reached out, her heart aching with the weight of the words she didn't want to hear. "Riven," she whispered, her voice breaking. She couldn't lose him—not like this. Not after everything they had been through. They had chosen love. They had chosen *each other*. And now, the world was asking her to choose again. To choose who would live and who would die.

And the cost was too high.

Her eyes searched the dark abyss before her, desperate, pleading. "Riven," she called again, her voice now filled with a strength she didn't know she had. "We've survived the darkness together. We'll survive this too."

The figure, looming before her, seemed to waver as the ground shook once again. "Your love is the key to the balance. But it is also the key to its destruction. Do not fight it. Let it go, or the world you have fought for will fall into chaos."

But Mirella knew, deep in her soul, that she couldn't. She

couldn't let go of the love they had fought so hard to protect. The world might demand balance, but love—*their love*—was worth fighting for.

She turned, her heart beating wildly, searching for Riven, for the bond that had always tied them together, stronger than any force, any shadow.

And in that moment, she felt it—his presence. His heart. It pulsed through the magic between them, a lifeline. He was still there, still alive. And together, they would face whatever this was.

They had not come this far to be torn apart.

Not now.

Not *ever*.

Mirella raised her hand to the sky, the magic within her swelling with renewed force. The stars above flickered again, and the earth seemed to grow still. "We are one," she said, her voice strong. "And we will not fall."

The darkness around her began to pull back as Riven's presence surged beside her, his heart beating in time with hers. Together, they would defy the Circle.

They would rewrite their fate. Together.

Seventeen

The Final Dawn

T he night was suffocating, a heavy, oppressive blanket that seemed to hold the world in its grip. The moon, once a guiding light through their darkest hours, now hung low and uncertain, a pale, sickly reflection of the light it had once held. The stars, scattered across the sky like shards of broken glass, flickered weakly, their light dimmed by the force that lingered just beyond the veil of the world. The earth, once so alive with the hum of magic, now felt cold, distant, as if it, too, were holding its breath.

Mirella stood on the precipice of the final trial, the wind whipping through her hair, her heart pounding in her chest as she gazed out at the vast expanse of the land before her. The mountains loomed like silent giants in the distance, the forests stretched endlessly to the horizon, but all of it felt wrong. The air was thick with an ancient energy, the final remnant of the curse that had sought to destroy everything. The shadows that had once been confined to the corners of their lives now clawed at the edges of reality, threatening to tear everything apart.

And yet, amidst the growing darkness, she felt something else—a flicker, like the first spark of a flame in the cold. Riven stood beside her, his hand finding hers, their fingers entwining with an unspoken promise. His presence was a steadying force, grounding her in the chaos of the world around them. They had fought together for so long. They had endured so much. And now, standing at the edge of everything, they would face this final challenge together.

Riven turned to her, his face solemn but filled with a quiet strength that made her believe—truly believe—that they could overcome anything. He had always been her anchor, her guide, and now, as the weight of their final task settled upon them, it was clearer than ever: *They were one.*

"Mirella," Riven said softly, his voice a low murmur in the chaos of their thoughts. "Are you ready?"

Mirella nodded, though the weight of the question pressed down on her chest. *Ready?* How could she be ready for what was about to come? How could anyone be ready to face the culmination of their entire existence—the choice that would either redeem the world or condemn it forever?

But she wasn't facing it alone. Not this time.

"I'm ready," she whispered back, squeezing his hand in reassurance. "Together."

A sharp crack of thunder echoed through the sky, the storm that had been building for hours now breaking wide open, releasing its fury upon the land. The wind howled, the earth trembled beneath their feet as if it, too, was protesting the enormity of the coming battle. But they had no choice. The final manifestation of the curse was here—alive, breathing, and ready to tear the world apart if they failed.

They moved forward, stepping into the clearing where the heart of the world had once pulsed with life and magic. But now, it was empty—silent and cold, like the hollow remnants of what had once been. The ground was cracked and blackened, the once-vibrant earth now tainted by the last traces of the curse. In the center of the clearing, a dark figure emerged from the shadows, its form shifting and shifting again as though it were not bound by the same laws that governed the world.

The Night King. The very embodiment of everything they had fought against.

But he was different now—no longer the man he had once been. The curse had changed him, twisted him into something far darker, something beyond their understanding. His eyes gleamed with malice as he took a step toward them, his presence radiating an unbearable weight of power.

"You've come," the Night King said, his voice low and guttural. "The last ones to face the truth. You've broken the curse, you've tried to heal the world, but do you truly understand the price of your actions? The balance you have disrupted cannot simply be restored with magic. You cannot rewrite the stars, Mirella, Riven. The world *will* fall. It *must* fall."

Mirella's heart tightened as she felt the darkness swirl around her, the oppressive weight of his words sinking deep into her chest. The truth of what they had done—the truth that the curse was never truly broken, that the cycle had never truly ended—threatened to crush them both. But they had no time to dwell on it. They had come too far to turn back now.

The Night King laughed softly, his voice a cruel whisper in

the stillness of the clearing. "You think you can stop me? You think your love, your bond, can heal what has been broken for eons? You are fools. *This* is the price. *You* are the price."

Mirella felt Riven's grip on her hand tighten, his presence beside her like a fire against the cold shadows. She turned to him, her gaze steady and filled with a quiet resolve. They had made it this far, and they would make it through this final trial. Their love, their bond, was the key. It always had been.

The Night King raised his hand, and the sky darkened further, the storm gathering with a ferocity that made the very air crackle with energy. The ground shook, the air grew heavy, and a terrible, unnatural silence fell over the clearing.

"It's time," the Night King said, his voice filled with malice. "Let us see if your love is truly enough. Let us see if it can withstand the curse you've both awakened."

The world seemed to bend around them as the curse manifested in full, its power surging like a tidal wave, crashing over them. Mirella and Riven were thrown back by the force, their bodies slamming into the ground. The energy of the curse burned through their veins, sharp and hot, threatening to tear them apart.

But they fought it. Together.

Mirella pushed herself up, her heart pounding, her breath coming in ragged gasps. The magic within her—both light and shadow—flickered like a flame on the verge of extinguishing. But it was *their* flame. The one they had nurtured, the one they had protected. And as long as they held onto that, they could not fail.

Riven was beside her, his sword drawn, his eyes locked on the Night King. The air between them hummed with a raw, electric tension.

"Do you understand now, Mirella?" the Night King sneered. "Do you see what I am? What we are? You cannot stop the cycle. It is endless. You are bound to it, as much as I am."

Mirella turned to Riven, her voice steady despite the storm of energy swirling around them. "We are not bound to you, or to anyone," she said. "We are bound to each other."

With that, she reached out, her hands glowing with silver light, her magic surging through her. The bond between them flared, a radiant, blinding pulse of energy that exploded outward, pushing back against the curse, against the darkness.

The Night King screamed in agony, his form flickering as the magic clashed with his own, fighting against the darkness that had long consumed him.

Mirella's chest tightened as she pressed her hands together, drawing on every last ounce of strength she had. Riven stood beside her, his sword raised, his body moving in rhythm with her, their magic intertwining in a way that made the very air hum with power.

And in that moment, Mirella knew—this was the final test. The ultimate sacrifice. Their love was the key to breaking the cycle, but it would come at a cost.

Riven turned to her, his eyes filled with unspoken words. *We've come this far. Whatever happens, I'm with you.*

She nodded, her heart swelling with the truth of it. Together, they could face anything. Together, they could stop the cycle. Together, they could save the world.

With a final, unified cry, they unleashed everything—their love, their magic, their strength—into the curse.

The world exploded in light.

The Night King screamed, his form disintegrating into the darkness, as the very fabric of reality tore itself apart. The ground shook violently, the storm above them reaching its peak, but the light they wielded, their bond, their love, pushed through it all, unraveling the curse that had held the world in its grip for so long.

And then, as the light faded, the storm began to calm. The earth stilled beneath them. The darkness retreated.

For the first time, in what felt like an eternity, the world was at peace.

Mirella fell to her knees, breathless, her body exhausted, but alive. Riven was beside her, his hand on her shoulder, his face pale but filled with relief. Their bond, though tested, had not broken. It had been forged in the fires of sacrifice, and it would remain unshakable.

"We did it," Riven whispered, his voice hoarse. "We're free."

Mirella's heart swelled with emotion as she looked up at the sky. The storm clouds were gone, replaced by the soft, warm light of dawn. The first rays of the sun touched the earth, painting the world in a golden glow. For the first time in what felt like forever, the land was whole again.

Together, they had restored balance. Together, they had broken the curse.

And as they stood there, hand in hand, the first light of dawn breaking through the darkness, they knew that their love would live forever, no matter the outcome. The world would always change, but their bond would remain.

And in that moment, beneath the silver moon and the rising sun, they were free.

The light of the rising sun bathed the land in soft, golden hues, casting away the remnants of the storm that had battered the earth. Mirella sat on the ground, her body exhausted but filled with a quiet satisfaction, as if the very bones of the world had sighed in relief. The winds, once fierce and howling, now seemed to murmur softly, carrying with them the promise of peace.

Beside her, Riven remained kneeling, his hand resting on the earth, his fingers lightly touching the cracked soil. His expression was one of quiet wonder, his eyes scanning the sky as the last shadows of the Night King's power dissolved. There was no sign of the storm anymore, no sign of the overwhelming darkness that had once consumed the world. The land was healing, the magic that had once been broken now stabilizing.

But even as the peace began to settle over them, the silence of the world around them felt strangely final.

The curse was broken. The Night King was gone. The cycle of darkness had ended, but the cost… the cost was more than either of them had truly understood.

Riven turned toward Mirella, his eyes searching hers as if he were seeing her for the first time. The weight of their shared sacrifice hung heavily between them, yet there was something else—something that wasn't burdened by the past. Their love, still glowing beneath the surface, felt renewed, like a flame that had been fanned back to life after it had been nearly smothered.

"You're still here," he said, his voice rough, filled with disbelief. "We're both still here."

Mirella smiled, the exhaustion in her bones pulling at her, but it was a deep, satisfying kind of weariness. "We are."

His hand found hers, their fingers intertwining as the world around them began to settle. It was as if the land itself were drawing in a deep breath, absorbing the magic they had unleashed into it. She could feel it—there was something tangible now in the air, a gentle pulse of power that resonated through her, not from a curse, but from the balance they had restored. And though she had felt the weight of the world press against her before, she now felt lighter, as though something had been lifted from her heart.

"But what now?" Mirella whispered, her voice soft with the lingering doubt that still clung to her. "What happens to us? To the world?"

Riven glanced at her, his expression one of quiet understanding. "I think we rebuild," he said, his voice steady. "Everything we've fought for. Everything we've lost, we rebuild."

Mirella nodded, her eyes scanning the horizon, where the first tendrils of light stretched across the land. She could see the scars of the battle, the places where the earth had cracked and broken under the weight of the curse. But beneath it all, there was a new vitality beginning to show itself—small signs of life creeping back into the land.

"It will take time," she murmured. "But I think we can do it. Together."

Riven squeezed her hand. "We already have."

The world was still in its infancy, recovering from the darkness that had held it in its thrall for so long. The magic that had flowed through them had not only broken the curse, but it had also restored the flow of life to the world. It was subtle, almost imperceptible to the naked eye, but there was a shift in the very air—the land breathed again.

"We'll need help," Mirella said, her mind racing with the possibilities. "There are people who need guidance. The world has been in chaos for so long. We need to show them how to live without the weight of the curse hanging over them."

Riven nodded, his gaze thoughtful. "We'll rebuild. But we can't do it alone. There are others—those who fought with us. The Keepers of the Veil, the allies we made along the way. They can help. Together, we can restore the balance of life. We can teach them."

Mirella turned to him, her heart swelling at his words. "And what about us? What happens to us now? Are we… free?"

Riven met her gaze, his eyes filled with a quiet intensity. "We've always been free. Even when the curse tried to control us, we fought to choose our own destiny. Now, we've earned that freedom. It's ours. And I won't let anything—*anyone*—take it away from us."

She smiled, her heart lightening with the truth of his words. They were free. Not just of the curse, not just of the darkness that had sought to consume them, but free to choose who they were, to choose the future they wanted to build together.

"Then let's build it," she whispered.

The light of the sun grew stronger, warming the earth beneath them, and Mirella could feel the magic in the air shift, as if acknowledging their promise. Together, they would build a new world—not one defined by the curse, but one born from the love that had overcome it.

As they stood, side by side, their hands still clasped, the land around them seemed to come alive. The trees that had once been barren now showed signs of new growth, their leaves budding with fresh green. Flowers bloomed at their feet, and the air grew thick with the scent of new life. The world was healing—slowly, but surely. The sky above them shifted from a pale blue to a vibrant, deep shade of indigo, as if the heavens themselves were acknowledging the new dawn.

"You know," Mirella said, her voice soft, "there's still so much to do. We have to help those who were affected by the darkness. The villages, the lands that were ravaged… they need rebuilding. And the people…"

Riven nodded, his eyes steady, his voice filled with resolve. "We'll help them. But not just with magic. With love. With patience. We'll show them how to live with hope again."

As they stood together, watching the first rays of the new dawn break over the horizon, Mirella felt a surge of warmth and light. The past, the darkness, the curse—it was all behind them now. The road ahead was uncertain, but it was theirs to walk. Together.

Their love had been the key. And now, it would be the foundation on which they built the world anew.

"Together," Mirella said softly, looking up at him.

Riven smiled, his hand tightening around hers. "Always."

And in that moment, beneath the light of the silver moon that had witnessed their battles and sacrifices, and beneath the first light of the dawn that heralded the new world, they knew that their journey was far from over. It was just beginning.

Together, they would face whatever came next—no matter the challenge, no matter the cost. For their love was stronger than any darkness, and it would guide them into the future, into the light. The circle had been broken, and a new path had begun.

The final dawn had arrived. And they, together, were its dawn.

Eighteen

The New Dawn

❦

The world had changed.

Mirella stood at the edge of the cliff, her breath catching in her throat as she looked out over the horizon. The first rays of the sun were breaking through the dissipating clouds, casting the earth below in soft hues of amber and gold. It was the dawn of a new era, a world that had been born from the ashes of the old, a world they had fought for, bled for, sacrificed for. The darkness that had clung to the land for so long was now a memory—a shadow fading in the light.

And yet, even as the world around her bloomed with new life, Mirella could feel the remnants of the battle still lingering in the air—the weight of everything they had endured, the sacrifices they had made. She could hear the soft wind rustling through the trees, the faint song of the birds returning to the skies, but it was not the sound of victory that filled her heart—it was the echo of what had been lost.

Riven's presence beside her grounded her, his steady hand finding hers as he stood just behind her, watching the same horizon. She could feel the warmth of his touch, the strength in his fingers, a reminder that, despite everything, they had made it. They had survived the darkness, and they had shaped a future together.

Mirella turned to face him, her heart swelling at the sight of his face, his eyes still as dark and fierce as they had been the day they first met. The shadow of the curse was gone, but in its place was a quiet storm—a storm of emotions, of love, of hope, of loss. They had come so far, and yet the road ahead was still uncertain.

"You've always been the light," she said softly, her voice trembling with the weight of her words. "Even in the darkest of times."

Riven's lips quirked upward, his eyes never leaving hers. "So have you. Together, we've always been more than just light and shadow. We've been *us*."

Mirella smiled, feeling the truth of his words settle deep in her chest. They had faced the world's greatest darkness— together. And together, they had torn it apart.

But it wasn't just the curse they had broken—it was a world that had been fractured, a future that had been set on a path of destruction. The price had been steep, the journey long, but in the end, it had been their love that had reshaped everything. Their love had been the key, the magic that had not only freed them, but had forged a new reality, a new world where the shadows no longer held sway.

Riven squeezed her hand, the gesture simple but filled with the weight of everything they had shared. "We've changed the world, Mirella," he said, his voice rough with emotion. "But now, we have to live in it."

She nodded, feeling the weight of his words as they settled in her heart. They had fought to restore balance, to rewrite the fate of a world consumed by darkness. But now, with the war won, with the curse broken, they were left with a world to rebuild—and to rebuild it, they would have to face the future, a future that had been written in the ashes of the past.

"Do you think it's possible?" she asked, her voice barely a whisper. "To create something new? To make a world where love truly triumphs over the darkness?"

Riven's gaze softened, and for a moment, Mirella saw the weariness in his eyes. The battles, the losses, the uncertainty—they had all taken their toll on him. And yet, in his eyes, there was something more—a quiet, unshakable belief.

"We've already started," he said, his voice steady. "Look around you, Mirella. The land is healing. The people are rebuilding. There is hope now. There is life. We just have to keep going. Together."

Mirella looked out at the landscape before them. The fields stretched out into the distance, lush with the beginnings of new growth. The trees, once stripped of their leaves by the curse, were now filled with vibrant green, their branches reaching up toward the sky, as if to touch the heavens themselves. The river, which had once run dark and stagnant, now flowed with clear, shimmering water, reflecting the first light of the sun.

The world was healing.

But it was not just the world that was healing—it was them.

"I never thought this day would come," Mirella said softly, her voice tinged with wonder. "I never thought I'd see the end of it. The end of the curse, the end of the darkness. I thought… I thought it would always be there."

Riven's hand tightened around hers, his gaze never wavering. "We *were* part of the darkness. It was always inside us. But now, we're part of the light. It's not about erasing the past—it's about using it to create something better."

Mirella turned to him, her heart swelling with the love and admiration she had for this man—this warrior, this prince, this lover—who had fought beside her through the darkest of nights. They had been through so much together, and now, with the curse broken, they were free to write the next chapter of their lives.

The first rays of the sun bathed them in warmth, the golden light catching in Riven's dark hair, casting his face in a soft glow. His features, sharp and strong, seemed to soften in the light, and for a moment, Mirella could see the man who had once been lost to darkness. He was no longer defined by his curse. He was no longer just a prince, or a warrior. He was Riven. Her Riven.

"Mirella," he said, his voice low and filled with something that made her heart skip a beat. "There's nothing left to fear. Nothing left to fight."

Her heart fluttered in her chest. "But there's so much left to do," she replied, her voice filled with the weight of their responsibility. "The world needs us. The people need us."

He nodded, his expression filled with quiet understanding. "We don't have to do it alone. We have allies. We have friends. And we have each other."

Mirella's eyes filled with tears at the simplicity of his words. How had she not seen it before? The world had always been *about* them. But it wasn't just about them anymore—it was about everyone. It was about the love they had fought for, the love that had burned bright enough to drive back the darkness. And that love would continue, not just between them, but in the world they were rebuilding.

"We're not alone," she whispered, the truth of it filling her with a warmth that spread through her chest, into her very bones. She felt the weight of her power now—of the magic that flowed through her, that was part of her, but she also felt the deep, unshakeable truth: love was the greatest magic of all. Love had torn down the walls of the curse. Love had created the world anew.

Together, they would heal it.

The sun rose higher in the sky, its light flooding the land, washing over them both as they stood hand in hand, no longer burdened by the shadows of the past. The future stretched out before them, uncertain, yes—but full of promise. They had broken the curse, yes. But in its place, they had built something even more powerful—a legacy. A love that would endure.

And as the first light of the new day bathed the land in its golden glow, Mirella knew one thing for sure—no matter the storms that might come, no matter the trials they would face, love would always be the light in the darkness.

And with that thought, she turned to Riven, her heart soaring with hope.

"Let's build a future," she said, her voice filled with a quiet resolve. "Together."

Riven's smile was soft, but it was filled with everything they had fought for—the promise of a new world, a world where love would always triumph over darkness.

"Always," he replied, his voice steady and full of conviction.

And together, they stepped forward into the new dawn, ready to face whatever lay ahead, knowing that their love would forever be the foundation on which the world was rebuilt.

The morning light stretched further across the land, the golden rays kissing the earth as the sun climbed higher, casting a brilliance that felt both new and eternal. Mirella and Riven stood together at the edge of the cliff, their fingers still intertwined, gazing out over the vast expanse before them. They had stood in the face of unimaginable darkness, and now they stood at the dawn of a world reborn. There was no victory without sacrifice, no peace without struggle, and yet, in this quiet moment, it all felt worth it.

The wind carried the scent of fresh rain, mingling with the earthiness of new life. Mirella could feel it in her bones—the land was healing, the magic flowing again like it had once done, centuries ago, before the curse had taken hold. It was strange, but in a way, the world now felt like a canvas waiting to be painted, and they, both Mirella and Riven, were the ones who would determine what the next stroke would be.

"I never imagined this moment would feel so… still," Mirella said quietly, her voice reflecting the calm that surrounded them.

Riven shifted beside her, his gaze fixed on the horizon, but his presence was solid, unyielding beside her. "It's a strange thing, isn't it? After all the chaos, the battles… to feel this peace. This stillness."

Mirella glanced at him, noticing how the edges of his features had softened. The weight that had once been so heavy on him was now gone. He had been freed from the curse, but there was a quiet tension in his eyes—a new understanding that he had earned his place in this world, not as a soldier bound by fate, but as a man who had chosen to live by his own will.

And she knew, in that moment, that he was not just her partner in this new world—they were both the architects of it.

"You've changed, Riven," she said softly, her voice barely above a whisper. "We've both changed."

He turned to face her, his lips curving into a small, almost bittersweet smile. "I think we had to, Mirella. To survive, to overcome… But I don't think I mind. I'm not the man I was when I first met you."

"I'm glad," she replied, her words more genuine than she'd ever thought they could be. "Because I'm not the woman I was either."

She could feel the magic between them, the pulse of the land, the quiet rhythm of the earth that beat in sync with the power that flowed through her veins. She had always known she was connected to the world in ways that were difficult to describe, but now, after everything, she felt that connection more clearly than ever. And it was not just her magic that had changed—the curse had been a curse not only on the land but on their hearts. Now that it had been lifted, there was room for something new. Something brighter.

But even as she stood there, her hand in Riven's, the shadows that lingered in her heart reminded her that the cost of this peace had not been small. Though the world was healing, the scars of the past were still fresh. The people who had fought beside them, the lives they had touched, the lands that had been ravaged by war—none of that could be erased by a single sunrise.

"We've done something remarkable," Riven said after a long pause, as if reading her thoughts. "But it's not over. The world is healing, but it's up to us to guide it. To show them what it means to live in this new world."

Mirella nodded, her eyes narrowing as the weight of his words sank in. They had restored the balance, yes, but it was not the end of the story. There was much work to be done. The world would need their leadership, their guidance. And perhaps more than anything, the people needed hope—real hope, not just the promise of a world that could heal, but the tangible steps to rebuild it.

"I know," she said, a fire growing in her chest. "And we will. Together."

They both looked back at the horizon, where the sun's rays were beginning to spread across the land, chasing away the last remnants of darkness. It felt like the land was holding its breath, like the whole world was watching, waiting for what came next. The air was thick with the weight of their shared promise—the weight of everything they had survived, everything they had built. And the weight of the future.

"We'll need help," Riven said, his voice low but steady. "We can't do this alone."

Mirella turned to him, her expression serious. "I know. We'll need the Keepers, the allies who fought beside us. There are people who need healing, people who need guidance. There are places still scarred by the darkness."

"Then we rebuild," Riven said with quiet determination, his gaze never leaving the land below. "Not just the land. But the hearts of the people. We need to remind them that the light isn't something to fear—it's something to embrace."

Mirella squeezed his hand, feeling the weight of his words. "And we'll show them that even after all the darkness, love is still here. We'll teach them what it means to live without fear."

Riven turned to face her then, his eyes meeting hers with an intensity that made her heart skip a beat. "Together."

Mirella's heart swelled at the promise in his voice. She nodded, her fingers tightening around his.

"Together," she echoed.

As they stood there, side by side, the rising sun painting the world in shades of gold and pink, a soft breeze lifted Mirella's hair, carrying with it the scent of new beginnings. The world, despite everything, was still alive—still full of possibilities, full of hope.

And in that moment, Mirella knew something deeper than ever before: the world was not defined by the curse they had broken, nor the battles they had fought. It was defined by the choices they made, the love they shared, and the legacy they would leave behind.

The world was changing, but it was changing for the better. The night had ended. The dawn had come.

And it was their turn to walk into it.

Later that day, as the village began to stir to life, Mirella and Riven found themselves walking through the newly rebuilt streets. People were hard at work, rebuilding homes, tending to the fields, and beginning the long process of restoring everything that had been lost. The weight of what they had done was heavy, but so was the understanding that this was just the beginning. This world, their world, was theirs to create.

As they passed through the streets, the people who had once looked at them with fear and uncertainty now greeted them with warm smiles, offering thanks for the light they had brought. Their journey had not just changed the land—it had changed the hearts of the people. It had brought them together.

Mirella's heart swelled as she watched the people, working in harmony, rebuilding, reclaiming their lives. The scars of war still remained, but there was a sense of unity in the air, a feeling of possibility. A new day had arrived, and they were no longer shackled by the past.

"We did it," she murmured, her voice filled with awe.

Riven's arm brushed against hers as they walked. "No, *we* did it. Together."

And as they walked, hand in hand, through the heart of the village, they knew that their love had not only shaped the world—but that it would continue to shape it, to inspire it, for generations to come. The darkness had been vanquished, and in its place, love had blossomed like a flower, spreading across the land, its roots deep in the soil of the earth.

The new dawn had arrived.

And they, together, would see it through.

Nineteen

The Legacy of the Thorn

The years had passed like the turning of the seasons, slow yet inevitable. The world Mirella and Riven had fought to save had flourished, no longer bound by the curse that had once threatened to consume it. The fields, once burned and broken by war, now stretched green and golden beneath the warm embrace of the sun. Villages bustled with life, children laughing as they ran through cobblestone streets that had once been soaked in blood. The rivers flowed clear and strong, and the forests that had once held shadows darker than night now stood tall, their branches reaching toward the heavens like silent sentinels of a world reborn.

Yet, though time had softened the memory of the great war, the story of Mirella and Riven had not been forgotten.

Their tale had become legend.

It was spoken in hushed whispers by the fireside, recounted in epic poems sung by traveling minstrels, etched into the very fabric of history. In every town, in every kingdom, in every corner of the world they had saved, the story endured— a testament to love's defiance against the darkness, to the strength of two souls who had dared to challenge fate itself.

And though they were gone, their presence lingered.

In the rustling of the trees when the wind swept through the valley.

In the shimmering silver light of the moon as it illuminated the land they had freed.

In the quiet beating of every heart that still believed in love.

Deep within the heart of the kingdom, nestled between mountains that once harbored unspeakable darkness, stood the Silverthorn Sanctuary. It had been built on the land where the final battle had been fought, where Mirella and Riven had made their last stand against the Night King and the remnants of the curse.

Now, it was a place of peace.

The sanctuary's grand halls were carved from white stone, streaked with veins of silver that shimmered under the light of the moon. At its center, an enormous tree stood—the Silverthorn. Its bark was smooth as silk, its leaves a strange blend of green and silver, glowing faintly in the twilight. No one knew how it had come to be, only that it had sprouted on the very spot where Mirella and Riven had fallen after the final battle.

It was said that the tree bore their essence, that its roots carried whispers of their love, that its branches held the stories of all they had done. The people believed it was a gift from the heavens, a reminder that even in death, love could never truly fade.

On this night, beneath the silver glow of the tree's leaves, a young girl sat cross-legged in the grass, her golden eyes wide with wonder as she listened to the voice of her grandmother weaving the legend once more.

"Tell it again," the girl pleaded, gripping the edge of her shawl. "Tell me about the last battle."

The old woman chuckled, brushing a gentle hand over her granddaughter's dark curls. "Again? Haven't you heard this tale enough times?"

The girl shook her head vigorously. "I want to hear it the way you tell it."

The grandmother smiled, settling into her chair as the wind carried the scent of blooming night jasmine through the air. She let the silence stretch for a moment, savoring the weight of the story she was about to tell.

"Many years ago," she began, her voice a melody of wisdom and memory, "there was a time when the world was veiled in shadow. A time when the curse of the Night King threatened to consume all that was good, all that was light."

The little girl clutched her shawl tighter, eyes shimmering in the dim light. "And that's when they came, didn't they?" she whispered.

The old woman nodded. "Yes, child. That is when they came. Mirella, with magic as fierce as the moon itself, and Riven, the warrior bound by shadow and fate. Two souls who should have been enemies, but instead found something stronger than destiny itself."

"Love," the girl breathed, eyes alight.

"Love," her grandmother agreed. "A love so powerful, so enduring, that not even the darkest magic could break it."

The wind stirred the branches of the Silverthorn tree, and the old woman glanced up at it with reverence.

"They fought bravely," she continued. "Side by side, through endless night and unrelenting storm. They wielded not just magic, not just steel, but their very hearts. And in the final hour, when the Night King sought to claim the world as his own, Mirella and Riven gave everything."

She fell silent for a moment, letting the words settle. The child waited, breath held, as if the next part of the story would determine the fate of the world itself.

"They won," the old woman finally said. "But the victory was not without cost. The battle took from them their last breath, but in their place, they left something greater."

She gestured to the tree before them, its silver leaves rustling as if in acknowledgment. "This tree stands as proof of their love, of their sacrifice. It is said that when the wind moves through its branches, you can still hear their voices. And when the moonlight touches its bark, you can feel their warmth. They are not gone. They are everywhere."

The little girl looked up at the tree in awe, her small fingers brushing over the grass beneath her. "Do you think they can hear us?" she asked softly.

The old woman smiled. "Perhaps. Perhaps they listen to every heart that still believes in their story."

The girl was quiet for a long time, staring up at the sky. Then, she stood and walked toward the Silverthorn tree, pressing her small hand against its trunk.

And for the briefest moment, she swore she felt something—warmth, like a heartbeat, a steady and comforting pulse.

She turned back to her grandmother, eyes bright. "I want to be like them," she declared. "Brave, and kind, and strong."

The old woman chuckled, rising slowly from her chair. She placed a gentle hand on the child's shoulder, looking up at the tree with her. "Then remember, little one," she whispered, "true strength does not come from power or magic. It comes from love. It comes from the choices we make, the people we fight for, the light we carry even when the world grows dark."

The girl nodded, her small hands clenching into fists. "I'll remember."

The wind sighed through the branches of the Silverthorn tree, its leaves whispering their approval.

And somewhere, in the space between light and shadow, where love and legend intertwined, Mirella and Riven's story continued to be told.

Not as mere words.

Not as myth.

But as truth.

As legacy.

As love, eternal as the stars.

The night deepened around the Silverthorn Sanctuary, and the distant cry of an owl echoed through the quiet air. The firepit at the center of the village crackled softly, its light dancing over the faces of the gathered villagers who sat listening to the old woman's tale. The girl, still standing by the Silverthorn tree, felt an unshakable sense of connection—of something far beyond the world she had known, something that transcended time.

Her heart raced with a newfound understanding, a sense of purpose that pulsed through her like the magic the old woman spoke of. She didn't quite know what it meant yet, but she felt it in her bones. *One day,* she thought, *I'll share this story too. I'll carry it forward, just like they did.*

The gentle sway of the Silverthorn's branches in the wind

brought a sense of peace over her—a peace that would last beyond the fading moments of childhood, a peace that would echo for generations to come.

The child's thoughts swirled around her grandmother's words. *True strength comes from love.* Her small hand still rested against the silver-barked tree, and as her fingers traced the ridges of the wood, she felt an almost imperceptible hum, as if the tree itself was alive with energy, carrying the echoes of the love that had saved the world.

The voices of the villagers carried over from the firepit, stories of the past intermingling with songs of the future. The old woman's story had become a part of the collective memory, a song that everyone carried in their hearts, and the little girl knew it would never fade. Her eyes lifted to the moon overhead, shining like a beacon, her fingers still resting against the tree. *Mirella and Riven had shown them all what it meant to love fiercely,* she thought. *And that love would forever burn in the hearts of those who came after.*

But as she stood there, feeling the weight of history upon her, a soft murmur stirred the air around her, like the gentle rustling of the leaves, but deeper—more intimate. Her heart skipped, as though the world itself was whispering to her. Her hand pressed harder against the bark, as if she could somehow absorb the magic of it, the memory of it, all at once.

A sudden gust of wind caught the edges of her cloak, sending it fluttering about her legs. The leaves above rustled with a quiet intensity, like a soft sigh from the earth. For a fleeting second, the air seemed to thrum with an energy she couldn't quite place.

And then—she heard it.

A whisper.

It was faint at first, barely audible. But it was there.

The sound of a voice, soft and melodic, carried by the wind.

Her breath caught. The whisper seemed to grow louder, more distinct, but still gentle, as though it were coming from all directions.

"You are never alone," it said. "You are part of us. And we are part of you."

The girl's heart pounded in her chest as the whisper seemed to settle deeper into her being, like a secret only she was meant to understand. Her fingers tightened against the Silverthorn tree, and her thoughts rushed back to the stories she'd been told—stories of Mirella and Riven, of their love and sacrifice, of their fight against the darkness. Could it be?

"Mirella," she whispered into the night, as if calling for the very spirit of the past.

But there was no answer, only the moonlight and the rustle of the tree's branches in the wind.

And yet... the whisper lingered, a promise that the story would never end, that it would continue with every life it touched, in ways subtle and profound. The girl could feel it in the air, in the way the earth seemed to hum beneath her feet.

Her thoughts turned inward, connecting to the warmth inside her. She could feel the magic inside, a kind of quiet power that seemed to surge every time she thought of the tree. Every time she thought of Riven and Mirella.

She wasn't just standing in the shadow of a legend—she was part of it.

With a deep breath, she finally pulled away from the Silverthorn tree, but the sensation of the connection remained, thrumming through her like an unspoken bond. Her grandmother's voice echoed softly in her mind. *True strength comes from love.*

As she turned back to the firepit, where her family and the villagers sat, the stars overhead seemed to shine even brighter, as if their brilliance was a reflection of something that had been rekindled deep within her heart. She could feel the presence of those who had come before her—the warriors, the healers, the ones who had laid the foundation for this world. Mirella, Riven, and all the others whose stories had shaped the world they now inhabited.

And in the very air around her, she felt the legacy of the thorn—of the love that had bound them all together.

Her grandmother was still speaking, recounting the last days of the curse, the final moments when the Night King had been vanquished. But the child felt something deeper than words— she felt the weight of it, the history. The way the earth had been shaped by sacrifices long made.

She stepped forward, eager to join her grandmother and the others. The storyteller's eyes met hers, and for a moment, their gazes locked, a silent understanding passing between them. The girl understood now—it wasn't just the tale that mattered. It was the act of sharing it, of passing the torch. Each generation, each heartbeat, carried a piece of the story forward, whether or not they knew it.

"Grandmother," the girl said, her voice soft yet sure. "I will carry the story. I will tell it to the world."

Her grandmother's eyes softened, her lips curling into a gentle smile. "And you will tell it well, my child. Because the story lives in you, as it lives in all of us."

The fire crackled softly in the distance as the stars overhead continued their silent watch. The villagers spoke of the years to come—the peace that had been won, the world that had been saved. But in the center of it all, there was the Silverthorn, the tree that had grown from the love of two people who had sacrificed everything for the world. And it was here, beneath its glowing branches, that the next generation would rise to carry the legacy forward.

As the child sat back down with her family, she could feel it in the very air around her—the unbroken thread of history, of love, that stretched out across time. The whispers of Mirella and Riven, still strong, still guiding.

No matter how much time passed, the legacy of the thorn would never fade. It would live on in every story told, in every heart that beat with love, in every moment that carried with it the hope of a brighter future.

In the moonlight, the Silverthorn's leaves glowed faintly, as though it were still whispering, still alive with the energy of its origins.

And in the quiet moments between the crackling fire and the soft whispers of the wind, Mirella and Riven's love lived on.

A love that could never be extinguished.

A love that would forever shape the world.

Twenty

The End of the Curse

The earth had finally breathed.

It had been years since Mirella and Riven stood at the heart of their final battle, their love and sacrifice woven into the fabric of the world. The land, once ravaged by shadows, now stood untouched by darkness, the curse shattered, its hold released. The sky, once filled with the screech of the Night King's creatures and the weight of impending doom, was now a canvas of light and promise. The mountains that had once trembled beneath the weight of the evil that had seeped into every corner of the land now loomed proudly in the distance, their jagged peaks softened by the passage of time. Below them, life flourished.

But even in a world no longer gripped by the shadow of the curse, there was something that remained. A quiet, lingering presence that whispered through the wind—a reminder of the love that had bound the land together, the love that had transcended the curse and all that sought to tear it apart.

Mirella and Riven were gone, their bodies turned to dust long ago, but their love lived on. It lived in the very heartbeat of the earth, in the soil that was now rich and fertile, in the trees that reached toward the heavens, in the river that sang its way through valleys once blackened by evil. It lived in the hearts of the people who had once been lost to despair, who now held the memory of two souls who had defied destiny itself to save the world.

It was dusk when the travelers arrived at the Silverthorn Sanctuary.

The path up to the sanctuary was a winding road carved through the dense forest, where trees stood like guardians, their boughs heavy with the weight of centuries. Their leaves shimmered silver, catching the last of the sunlight as it dipped below the horizon. The air was thick with the scent of pine and earth, and the ground beneath their feet was soft with moss, as if the land itself had cushioned their steps.

A group of pilgrims had made the journey, just as generations before them had done, to pay homage to the legacy of Mirella and Riven. They walked in silence, their faces set with reverence, each person drawn not only by the legend but by the truth that something more than magic had shaped the world they now lived in. Something more than the battle they had fought against the curse. It had been love—love that had fueled their strength, that had built the foundation for peace.

The leader of the group, an elder named Caelus, walked at the front, his pace slow but steady, his eyes fixed on the distant outline of the Silverthorn tree. His hand rested lightly on the worn hilt of a sword—a relic from the old days, a token of a war long past. His thoughts, though filled with awe, were shadowed by something else—an unease that he could not shake.

"Do you feel it?" Caelus asked quietly, glancing over his shoulder at the young man walking behind him, a newcomer to the pilgrimage. "The weight of what lies ahead?"

The young man, whose face was still bright with the promise of youth, nodded, his hand resting over his chest. "I feel it," he replied, his voice filled with wonder. "The air is different here. It feels like… like it knows what has passed."

Caelus gave a soft laugh, his weathered face softening. "It does. The land remembers. The trees, the stones, the river—all of it remembers the love that saved it. And it will never forget."

As they drew closer to the sanctuary, Caelus's heart swelled with emotion. He had heard the stories, seen the old tapestries depicting the battle, felt the quiet hum of the legacy left behind. But even with all that he knew, standing here, at the threshold of where history had been written, he was overwhelmed by a sense of reverence.

Before them stood the Silverthorn tree, its bark glowing faintly in the twilight. Its branches stretched upward, twisting toward the heavens like an ancient hand reaching for the stars. The leaves shimmered with silver light, giving the entire tree an ethereal quality. It was a thing of beauty, yes, but also something more—something eternal, something that seemed to hold the memory of Mirella and Riven within its roots.

Caelus approached the tree, his steps measured, his breath steady. He reached out with trembling hands, touching the smooth bark, his fingers brushing over the veins of silver that ran through it. A shiver ran through him, as if the very act of touching the tree caused a ripple through time itself.

"It's here," the young man murmured, stepping up beside

him. "This is where they fell."

Caelus nodded. "Yes. This is where they fought their final battle. And this is where they left their mark on the world." His voice was thick with emotion, and his eyes softened as he looked up at the branches, now bathed in the pale light of the moon. "Their sacrifice was not in vain. It was a gift—to all of us."

There was a moment of silence, the quiet of the evening filling the space around them. The pilgrims stood together, hands clasped, eyes closed in remembrance.

The young man spoke again, his voice barely above a whisper. "Do you think they're still here?"

Caelus smiled faintly, his gaze still fixed on the Silverthorn tree. "In a way. Their love is a part of this land now, woven into every living thing. You'll see it for yourself as the years pass. Their story will be passed down, generation by generation. It will live on forever."

For a moment, they stood there, letting the silence wrap around them like a blanket, the weight of their words settling into the earth beneath their feet. The Silverthorn tree hummed with a quiet energy, its branches shifting as the wind passed through them, carrying the faint scent of jasmine and pine.

And then, as the last rays of sunlight disappeared beneath the horizon, the moon rose higher, casting its silver light over the sanctuary, illuminating the tree in a soft, glowing hue.

The pilgrimage had not just brought them here for the story— it had brought them here for the promise that love, even in its most difficult and heartbreaking forms, would always endure.

Elsewhere, across the lands that Mirella and Riven had saved, the legacy of their love continued to grow. The descendants of the people who had once lived in fear now carried the torch of the love that had broken the curse, the love that had freed the world.

In every village, in every city, in every corner of the kingdom, people gathered to celebrate not only the peace they now lived in, but the unshakable bond that had made it possible. Songs were sung, stories told, and every corner of the world bore the mark of their undying love.

And high above, where the stars twinkled with the brilliance of a thousand forgotten promises, the moon shone brighter than ever before. For every star in the sky, every flicker of light across the heavens, carried with it the story of Mirella and Riven.

Their love had shaped the world, and in turn, the world had shaped their love.

As time continued its endless march, their story became more than just a memory. It became a beacon, a guiding light for all those who believed. Because the truth of it was clear: no darkness, no curse, no evil force could ever extinguish the light of true love.

Mirella and Riven had given everything for the world. And now, the world would give everything back to them, every heart that beat, every life that flourished, a reminder that love— no matter the cost—would always find a way.

The Silverthorn tree stood as a testament to their love. And every evening, when the moon rose high and the stars began their quiet dance across the sky, the land still felt the echo of their hearts.

A love that could never die.

A love that would always endure.

And in the whispers of the wind, in the soft glow of the moon, the story of Mirella and Riven continued to live on—a legacy written in the very fabric of the earth, and a beacon for generations to come.

The night deepened, and the pilgrims remained by the Silverthorn tree, gathered beneath the vast expanse of the starlit sky. The whispers of the land swirled around them, faint echoes of the past intertwined with the present, as if the very world itself was alive with the memory of two souls who had loved beyond the bounds of time. In the quiet between each heartbeat, there was the pulse of eternity—a pulse that resided within the land, within the hearts of those who had lived and died in the wake of Mirella and Riven's sacrifice.

The Silverthorn tree, glowing in the moonlight, stood as a silent witness to everything that had come before and everything that would come after. It had grown from the earth where Mirella and Riven had given their lives, and from it sprouted the continuation of their legacy—a legacy that could never be erased.

Caclus, standing at the base of the tree, felt the weight of those generations pressing upon him. The children of this land, the future of their people, would carry the story of Mirella and Riven with them, not only in the words they spoke, but in their actions, in their love. Caelus, too, had lived through the curse and the war. He remembered the time before the breaking of the curse, the fear that had gripped every village, every heart, and the uncertain hope that had bloomed only after the battle had been won. He had been one of the first to stand beneath the Silverthorn tree, one of the first to witness the rebirth of the world.

He had thought that time would erase the pain, that it would dull the memory of their sacrifice, but instead, it had only amplified the truth: love was immortal.

With the moonlight bathing his face, Caelus knelt before the tree, placing a single white rose at its roots. It was a ritual he had performed every year, a simple act of gratitude, of remembrance. The rose symbolized the purity of their love—bright, untainted, and lasting.

The group stood in silence, the weight of the years pressing down upon them as the breeze shifted, carrying with it the scent of the flowers that bloomed at the foot of the Silverthorn. The wind seemed to carry something more, a hum in the air that was both familiar and new, as though the very fabric of the world was resonating with the energy of their love.

"Tonight, we honor not only the past," Caelus said softly, his voice breaking the stillness. "But the future. The future they fought to protect. Their love lives in all of us, in everything we touch. It is the foundation of our world, and it will continue to guide us, just as it guided them."

He paused for a moment, lifting his eyes to the stars. "We are their legacy. The people of this land, the children who will come after us—this peace, this light, it is because of them."

A deep silence followed, the only sound the whisper of the wind through the Silverthorn's branches, the faint murmurs of the pilgrims reflecting on the words they had just heard. They all felt it then—the deep connection to something far greater than themselves, to the history of the world, to the love that had transcended the boundaries of life and death. The stories of Mirella and Riven weren't just stories anymore; they were a part of the very fabric of the world, etched into the hearts of those who had come to understand the true meaning of love and sacrifice.

Caelus rose slowly, his heart heavy with the knowledge that

they would never fully understand all the ways in which their lives had been shaped by those who had come before. He stood, looking at the young man beside him, the next generation of those who would carry the story forward. The boy had yet to truly understand the weight of what was being asked of him, but Caelus knew he would—just as he had once learned.

The moon shone down upon them, its silver light glinting in the leaves above, and as the pilgrims began to disperse to their tents, Caelus remained for a moment longer, staring at the Silverthorn tree. It had been years, but it felt like only yesterday that he had first stood here, witnessing the birth of a new world.

The world is free, he thought. *The darkness is gone.*

And as he turned to leave, something shifted in the air—a subtle change, a feeling, as if the earth itself were breathing in sync with his heart. The magic was alive, vibrant, still pulsing beneath the surface of the land. Mirella and Riven's love had not only shaped the course of their world—it had bound it together, an unbreakable thread that would endure through the ages.

Caelus, now walking away from the Silverthorn Sanctuary, looked up at the night sky one last time. The stars twinkled above him, brighter than ever before. He could almost hear the whispers again—Mirella's voice, soft and gentle, Riven's deep, steady tone. It was as if they were watching from beyond the veil, their love still reaching out, still touching those who had inherited their story.

For a moment, he allowed himself to believe it. That they were there, still guiding him, still guiding them all.

And then, with one last glance at the Silverthorn tree, Caelus turned toward the path that led back to the village, the faces of the people they had saved—of the children who would grow up hearing the stories, of the land that had been healed—his heart filled with a quiet, hopeful peace.

The curse was gone. The darkness had been vanquished.

Mirella and Riven had given everything. And in return, the world was free.

And so, as time continued its unyielding march, the memory of their love—unbroken, eternal—lived on.

For love, no matter the cost, would always find a way.

Years passed, seasons turned. New generations were born, and the legend of Mirella and Riven was passed down, from one person to the next, from one heart to another. They became a story that echoed in every corner of the world, a tale told in whispers and songs. Their love was no longer just a memory—it was a living, breathing thing, carried forward by every act of kindness, every act of love.

And in the whispers of the wind, the soft glow of the moon, and the hearts of those who dared to believe, Mirella and Riven's legacy endured.

Their love, eternal as the stars, would never fade.

And the world, forever touched by it, would continue to shine.

The end.